This month, in

THE PLAYBOY MEETS HIS MATCH
by Sara Orwig

Meet Jason Windover—drop-dead gorgeous
cowboy and steadfast bachelor, at least until fiery
Meredith Silver knocks him head over
heels...*literally*. Can the notorious playboy
convince Meredith of his change of heart?

**SILHOUETTE DESIRE
IS PROUD TO PRESENT THE**

TEXAS
Cattleman's Club
The Last Bachelor

**Five wealthy Texas bachelors—all members of
the state's most exclusive club—set out to
uncover the traitor in their midst...
and find true love.**

* * *

And don't miss
THE BACHELOR TAKES A WIFE
by Jackie Merritt;
The final installment of the
Texas Cattleman's Club: The Last Bachelor series.
Available next month in Silhouette Desire!

Dear Reader,

Looking for romances with a healthy dose of passion? Don't miss Silhouette Desire's red-hot May lineup of passionate, powerful and provocative love stories!

Start with our MAN OF THE MONTH, *His Majesty, M.D.*, by bestselling author Leanne Banks. This latest title in the ROYAL DUMONTS miniseries features an explosive engagement of convenience between a reluctant royal and a determined heiress. Then, in Kate Little's *Plain Jane & Doctor Dad*, the new installment of Desire's continuity series DYNASTIES: THE CONNELLYS, a rugged Connelly sweeps a pregnant heroine off her feet.

A brooding cowboy learns about love and family in *Taming Blackhawk*, a SECRETS! title by Barbara McCauley. Reader favorite Sara Orwig offers a brand-new title in the exciting TEXAS CATTLEMAN'S CLUB: THE LAST BACHELOR series. In *The Playboy Meets His Match*, enemies become lovers and then some.

A sexy single mom is partnered with a lonesome rancher in Kathie DeNosky's *Cassie's Cowboy Daddy*. And in Anne Marie Winston's *Billionaire Bachelors: Garrett*, sparks fly when a tycoon shares a cabin with the woman he believes was his stepfather's mistress.

Bring passion into your life this month by indulging in all six of these sensual sizzlers.

Enjoy!

Joan Marlow Golan

Joan Marlow Golan
Senior Editor, Silhouette Desire

Please address questions and book requests to:
Silhouette Reader Service
U.S.: 3010 Walden Ave., P.O. Box 1325, Buffalo, NY 14269
Canadian: P.O. Box 609, Fort Erie, Ont. L2A 5X3

The Playboy Meets His Match

SARA ORWIG

Published by Silhouette Books

America's Publisher of Contemporary Romance

Special thanks and acknowledgment are given to Sara Orwig
for her contribution to the
TEXAS CATTLEMAN'S CLUB:
THE LAST BACHELOR series.

With thanks to Joan Golan and Stephanie Maurer.
Also, to all New Yorkers, God bless…

SILHOUETTE BOOKS

ISBN 0-373-76438-3

THE PLAYBOY MEETS HIS MATCH

Visit Silhouette at www.eHarlequin.com

Printed in U.S.A.

Books by Sara Orwig

Silhouette Desire

Falcon's Lair #938
The Bride's Choice #1019
A Baby for Mommy #1060
Babes in Arms #1094
Her Torrid Temporary Marriage #1125
The Consummate Cowboy #1164
The Cowboy's Seductive Proposal #1192
World's Most Eligible Texan #1346
Cowboy's Secret Child #1368
The Playboy Meets His Match #1438

Silhouette Intimate Moments

Hide in Plain Sight #679
Galahad in Blue Jeans #971

SARA ORWIG

lives with her husband and children in Oklahoma. She has a patient husband who will take her on research trips, anywhere from big cities to old forts. She is an avid collector of Western history books. With a master's degree in English, Sara writes historical romance, mainstream fiction and contemporary romance. Books are beloved treasures that take Sara to magical worlds, and she loves both reading and writing them.

"What's Happening in Royal?"

NEWS FLASH, May—The Texas Cattleman's Club annual ball is back on! Sebastian Wescott has announced his plans to reschedule the gala event for next month. The eligible ladies in town had better hurry if they want to snare a date—lately it seems like bachelors have become an endangered species around Royal....

In fact, no bachelor is safe, not even notorious playboy Jason Windover! Seems he's only had eyes for a fire-haired newcomer to town, Ms. Meredith Silver. If Jason is out to win the heart of that little lady, he may have bitten off more than he can chew—from what we hear, Ms. Silver packs quite a punch!

With Sebastian cleared of murder, the question on everyone's mind is: Who *really* murdered Eric Chambers? There have been quite a few closed-door meetings at the Texas Cattleman's Club lately. Could Royal's favorite gents have some suspicion as to the murderer's identity? If they do, they're not saying anything....

One

"**D**on't tell me I'm the club expert at seduction," Jason Windover grumbled good-naturedly, glancing around the circle of friends and fellow members of the Texas Cattleman's Club as they sat in one of the elegant private meeting rooms. Thick carpets, dark paneling and polished wood flooring graced the spacious room, built over ninety years earlier. A boar's head was mounted above the stone mantel, and a Tiffany chandelier glittered brightly.

The Texas Cattleman's Club was one of Texas's oldest and most exclusive clubs. Usually, it was a place where Jason could relax and enjoy his friends, but at the moment he was mildly annoyed. He crossed his jeans-clad legs, resting one booted foot on his knee, and arched his brows.

"*Au contraire,*" Sebastian Wescott said, turning to his longtime friend. "You're the one who excels at seduction, so I nominate you to get this Valkyrie out of our hair."

"I second that motion," snapped black-haired Will Bradford, a partner of Wescott Oil Enterprises.

Jason looked into Sebastian's silver-gray eyes and shook his head. "If nothing else, she's not my type," Jason said coolly, certain this foolishness would pass. "I like tall, long-legged, sophisticated blondes. Beautiful blondes who are poised and sexy. This wildcat sounds like five feet of pure trouble and anything but sophisticated, sexy or poised. Forget it, guys. It ain't gonna happen."

"The woman is unhinged. She belongs in a mental hospital," Dorian Brady added sharply. "She's got this vendetta against me—at the moment it's me. No telling who it will be tomorrow. She's mentally unstable, and her fixation could switch to any one of you. Lord knows, I haven't done the wild things she's accusing me of."

Studying Dorian, Jason felt cold distaste. Other than Dorian, Jason liked all the members of the Texas Cattleman's Club, an exclusive, prestigious facade which allowed members to work together covertly on secret missions to save innocents' lives. While most of the men had grown up in and around Royal, Texas, Dorian was a relative newcomer. There was an arrogance about Dorian that rankled him, but Jason knew he needed to get over his dislike. Dorian was, after all, Seb's half brother.

"You're elected," Rob Cole said dryly to Jason. "You're the rodeo guy. You can handle wild bulls and wild horses. I'm sure you can handle a wild woman."

"You're the detective—you should know how to handle her."

"Nope. You have a way with women, and I already have my hands full trying to find out what I can about our unsolved murder here in Royal." Rob studied the circle of men. "We have someone trying to frame Sebastian for the murder of Eric Chambers. We don't need this woman in our hair while we're trying to find out who's behind this."

"I wasn't here when she burst in on y'all, but I've heard what an unholy commotion she caused here at the club. Dammit, don't dump this on me." All of the men looked at Jason. "C'mon, y'all," Jason argued.

"You have to be the one," Sebastian replied. "You're the CIA-trained operative, so you've dealt with difficult people before. Frankly, I've been through enough lately, and I have a new bride to devote myself to."

Jason sighed and waved his hand. "Save your excuses. I can guess all of them. All right. I'll try to keep the little wildcat out of our hair."

"That problem solved, let's adjourn to poker," Keith, the computer expert, suggested, his brown eyes twinkling.

The men agreed swiftly, and Jason knew the matter was settled. Morosely, he joined them, getting a fresh drink, going through the motions while he contemplated his assignment. He didn't like one thing about it. He was not accustomed to forcing a female to do something she didn't want to do—in this case, he was going to have to do exactly that in order to keep this little wildcat out of the other guys' ways.

Will, Rob and Sebastian were all recently married. Marriage had become an epidemic, except he was safe—no marriage for him—at the moment there wasn't even a woman in his life. Maybe Keith should be the one to take care of this nuisance. Jason wondered whether Keith had ever gotten over his old flame, Andrea O'Rourke. He said he had, but he sure didn't act like it. Jason sighed. He could understand why this assignment had been dumped on him, but he didn't like it. Thank goodness he wasn't involved with anyone right now because this would be a very unwanted complication in his life. He wished he could just haul this Ms. Silver down to jail and ask Sheriff Escobar to lock her up and throw away the key until all their mysteries were solved.

When Jason realized he was losing the first round of the poker game, he shifted his thoughts to cards and forgot about Meredith Silver, hoping she had left town and he would never have to deal with her.

It was almost midnight when Jason pocketed his winnings and told his friends goodbye. Stepping outside, he inhaled the cool May air. A silver moon hung in the inky sky while stars were blotted out by the lights of the parking lot. As he crossed the lot to his black pickup, Jason's boot heels scraped the asphalt. As he reached for the door handle of his pickup, he heard a faint sound behind him.

The hairs on the back of Jason's neck prickled, and he stood motionless beside his pickup. His experience in the CIA had trained him to be a keen observer, and he knew he had heard the scrape of a footstep on the asphalt.

Jason stood in a row of empty cars and pickups. When he had walked from the clubhouse, there hadn't been another person in sight. In spite of the seemingly empty lot, Jason doubted he was alone in the parking lot. Should he look under the next car? he wondered, or would it be better to try to discover what the person intended? Jason pocketed his keys and headed casually back to the club.

He went through the front door, down a hallway past the cloakroom and rest rooms, and cut through the giant kitchen, touching the brim of his Stetson with his finger in silent greeting to the skeleton cooking crew still on duty at this late hour. They were familiar with the members of the club, and none of them questioned his presence in the kitchen as he passed through and went out a side door. He stepped into a flower bed, creeping behind cedars and flowering crape myrtles. Glad now that he had worn a dark blue Western shirt and his dark jeans, he moved stealthily even though he was wearing Western boots. He paused, his gaze sweeping over the empty lot and then settling on the car parked next to his.

He knew to whom it belonged—Dorian. As he watched, a shadow separated itself from the darker ones around it. Jason focused on a black-clad figure that had slithered out from beneath Dorian's car and now knelt beside the back tire.

Something glinted in the moonlight. There was a clunk and then a swift hiss of air. When the vandal moved to the front tire, Jason sprinted from his hiding place, determined to catch the rascal who was vandalizing club member's tires in their private parking lot.

Seeing Jason, the culprit dropped the knife and ran. From the short stature, Jason decided it was a teen. Jason's long legs gave him the advantage, and he stretched out his stride. As they raced across the lot, Jason made a flying tackle, wrapping his arms around the miscreant's tiny waist.

"Gotcha!" he snapped triumphantly as they both went crashing to the asphalt.

The high yelp didn't indicate anything about the vandal, but the moment they landed on the asphalt, and he felt the soft, curvaceous body beneath his, surprise rippled through Jason. A female! And then he guessed who it was. The crazy woman who was stalking his fellow club member, Dorian Brady—the wildcat who was his assignment.

"Oh, damn," he muttered. Never in his life had he hurt a woman and remorse filled him as he groaned and moved off her. "Are you all right?"

Light from one of the tall lamps spilled over him, although the brim of his hat shaded his face, but her back was to the lamp and her face was completely hidden. She was covered in black with a black cap and some black goop spread on her face, so that he couldn't distinguish her features. Jason hunkered down on the balls of his feet as she started to sit up.

Her fist shot out. Catching him completely by surprise, five feet of female did what few six-foot-plus, some-two-hundred-pounds of male had never done. Her blow landed squarely in his middle, knocking the breath from his lungs as she followed with a swift push that knocked him off balance. Springing to her feet, she tried to run for it.

Jason's surprise lasted only a second and then his natural reactions set in. He rolled forward, snaking his hand out, caught her by the ankle and yanked. For the second time in his life, he sent a female sprawling facedown.

He wasn't giving her another chance. Unceremoniously,

he grabbed his hat, scooped her up and slung her over his shoulder.

For someone who was up to criminal activities and packed a vicious punch for her size, her epithets and name-calling fit a five-year-old's vocabulary. Heck, some five-year-olds could do better.

Ignoring her harmless blows on his back and her sputtering fury, Jason carried her to his pickup, unlocked the door and dumped her inside. Like a cat springing back into battle, she came up fighting, but he was ready this time.

Tossing his hat into the back with one hand, he clamped her wrists in a tight grip with his other hand, pinning her against the locked door and the seat with his body. In spite of her struggles, he became aware of several things at once: an enticing perfume, a body whose topside was even more curvaceous and soft than her backside, a wiry strength he wouldn't have believed possible and short, guttural moans of battle that made him think of something far removed from their struggle. Against all wisdom, he was curious and wanted to see what she looked like.

"You just slashed a club member's tire, and I can call the sheriff and have you hauled to jail."

"Go ahead and call, you warp-noggined manhandler," she snapped. "They can't put me in jail for slashing a tire. I'll call my lawyer."

"Why do I doubt you even have a lawyer? *Warp-noggined?*"

This was the Valkyrie who Dorian said had been stalking him. Jason had suspected Dorian had been stretching the truth a bit, but after the past few minutes, he decided the man had been correct. Everything about her seemed amateurish, and he didn't think there was a lawyer, a plan or much sense. From the few minutes of dealing with her, he figured he had a crazy person on his hands, or perhaps a woman emotionally unhinged by a man who had done her wrong. Was this some ex-lover of Dorian's, and he didn't want to admit it?

"Settle down, wildcat. Fighting won't do you any good. You're not catching me by surprise ever again."

In the darkness he could see her jaw lift in a stubborn gesture. "That's what you think. Let me go. I can charge you with assault—"

"Hardly," he stated dryly. "I just caught you in a criminal act." She wiggled, struggling to break free, but it was having a far different effect on him. Jason had been a longer time than usual between women. She was soft, curvaceous and she was squirming and gyrating against him. His body was pressed over hers, pinning her down, but she was doing things that were setting him on fire in spite of his annoyance.

"Wildcat, do you know what you're doing?" he rasped.

She stilled instantly, and he knew she had become aware of his natural male response to a warm, sweet-smelling female rubbing sensuously against him.

When he reached down with his free hand and unbuckled his belt, her struggles became wild. Swiftly, he yanked his belt free, bound her wrists together and secured her to the door handle. "I'm not going to hurt you. You're just not going anywhere. You've caused enough trouble around here. Now, you make a choice. I take you home with me— I lock you in a room by yourself for tonight. I have no evil intentions, I promise. Tomorrow you go on your way and get out of Royal. Or I can take you to the sheriff. You decide."

Why he was taking her home with him, he wasn't altogether certain about, except he had been assigned to keep her out of the way of the rest of the club members, and it was the best way to keep an eye on her.

She struggled, and Jason tightened his grip. "Look, you're just going to get yourself in deep trouble. There are laws against stalking someone—"

"Stalking! I'm not stalking that rotten lowlife varmint. He's mean and vindictive and dishonest."

Jason was intrigued. "I've given you a choice. Make

your decision. Or it'll be the sheriff because I'd be glad to dump you into someone else's lap.''

They were both breathing hard—his ragged breath was not from exertion. Erotic thoughts were tempting him and she was the cause. She might be five feet of trouble, but she was definitely all woman and a very sweet-smelling one at that. Jason fished a handkerchief from his pocket and began to wipe the black stuff off her forehead.

"How do I know you won't hurt me?" she asked so softly that he had to lean closer. And got another deep whiff of her perfume. A little pesky wildcat shouldn't wear seductive perfume.

"You have my word on it," he said, and she gave a bitter laugh. "The sheriff or my house," he repeated.

"Your house," she whispered, her breath sweet, lightly brushing his skin.

Keeping up his guard, he moved away and fished for his keys, starting the pickup. Now she was hunched into a ball in the corner between the door and the back of the seat. As he drove out of the lot, he glanced at her again. She looked pitiful all huddled over, but his bruised midriff warned him not to be taken in by appearances. This was not a cringing, frightened little waif. The wildcat had a punch that had knocked him flat.

Jason worked out over an hour every day. He shouldn't have been felled by a blow from a female of her size, and he vowed he would increase his workouts tomorrow.

He opened the glove compartment and pulled out a flask of whiskey, opening it and offering it to her. "Need a drink?"

"Now you want to get me drunk so you can have your way with me," she snarled.

"Great grief," he grumbled, wanting a stiff drink himself, but resisting, since he was driving.

"Where did you get your vocabulary—out of some 1920s dime novel? Outside of melodramas, I didn't know anyone used that phrase *have your way with me.*"

"You're too young yourself to know anything about 1920s dime novels, and I certainly don't. And you know full well what I meant."

"I gave you my word. You're not my type anyway."

"I can imagine your type."

He glanced at her again, his curiosity growing. Silence stretched between them as he drove down Main Street, Royal, Texas, the place where he had grown up and lived a good part of his life. "So, what type do you imagine I'd like?" he asked finally.

"Someone beautiful, sexy, sophisticated and easy. *Real* easy."

Amused, he looked at her, still unable to see anything except a huddle of black.

"You don't think I have any charm to win over someone who isn't easy?"

"You tackled me twice," she said in the same haughty, aloof tone that he could recall early grade-school teachers lecturing him with. "That isn't a winning approach."

"I wasn't trying a winning approach. I never intended seduction. I was trying to stop a criminal act. That's not a fair judgment of me," he remarked, amused by her in spite of his annoyance at being saddled with responsibility for keeping her away from the others.

He drove past Pine Valley, the exclusive, private-gated, residential community that held mansions, including one belonging to his family where his brother was currently residing. Jason could take her there, but he preferred her out on the Windover Ranch—far enough out of town so that she would have a hell of a hike if she decided to run away.

"It might be a good idea if we knew each other's names. I'm Jason Windover."

"I'm Meredith Silver," she said.

"Well, hi, Meredith. Where are you from?"

"I'm from Dallas," she said.

"And what do you do in Dallas?" he asked, slipping

into old patterns of interrogation, avoiding the hot topics or accusations.

"I'm a computer programmer. I'm a freelance consultant."

"Interesting profession—and gives you freedom to keep your own hours sometimes."

"Yes, it does," she answered while she stared out the window. "We're out of town."

"I'm taking you to the Windover family ranch."

"You're a cowboy?"

"Yes, I am. I've been with the government, but I recently retired to the ranch. So, Meredith, who's your current boyfriend?"

"There isn't one," she replied. "But I'll bet there's a woman in your life."

"As a matter of fact, there's not at present."

"I'm sure she's not far in the past and there's another lined up somewhere in the near future."

"Now why do you think that? You don't know me."

"You have that easygoing manner of a man accustomed to always having a female in his life."

"Do I really?" he asked, amused by her observations.

"You know darn well you do. You're also egotistical and overbearing."

"Golly gee whiz. I'll have to work on that."

"You can save the charm because it won't work on me."

"Now is that a challenge or what?" he asked, his voice dropping as he shot her a look.

"It's definitely not a challenge. Besides, I'm not your type remember?"

"Point taken." He drove quietly for a few minutes and then asked, "Do you have a hotel room in Royal or did you intend to drive back to Dallas tonight?"

"I'm staying at the Royalton Hotel," she replied, naming Royal's oldest and finest hotel.

"Do you still have family in Dallas?"

"Yes. My sisters and my mom are in Dallas. I have an older brother who's in Montana, I think."

"Silver," he said, remembering a stocky, wild guy from the rodeo circuit. "I've met a bull rider—Hank Silver."

"That's my brother," she said with what sounded like reluctance.

"Well, small world. He's a tough cowpoke. I'll bet that's where you got the punch you pack. You have a big family," he said, curious to see what she looked like. Her voice was soft, low and soothing. A sexy voice that didn't match her volatile personality. If he had talked to her on a telephone and hadn't seen her in person, he would have conjured up an entirely different type of woman in his mind. The voice definitely didn't fit a little five-foot wildcat with a vocabulary as old-fashioned as his grandmother's. Her enticing voice didn't fit someone who could deliver a jab that knocked the breath from your lungs. But with Hank Silver as an older brother, Jason could well imagine, she'd had to defend herself growing up. From what Jason could remember, Hank Silver was in trouble with the law more than once over barroom brawls.

"I have two older brothers," he said. "Ethan and Luke."

"That's nice," she said, not trying to hide her anger.
for the next hour they lapsed into silence, a new experience for Jason with a female.

Jason turned south between large posts with the Windover brand carved on the front of each one and drove swiftly along a hard-packed road until they pulled up behind the sprawling ranch house that had belonged to his family for four generations. Moonlight splashed over a combination of red sandstone, rough-hewn logs and glass. A porch with a sloping roof ran along the front and a well-tended lawn was surrounded by a picket fence. Beyond the house were outbuildings, a guest house, a bunkhouse and a barn.

Jason stopped near the back gate and untied the belt, taking her arm to lead her inside. When they entered the house, he switched on lights in a back entryway that held a coat rack, pictures of horses and potted plants. He turned and punched buttons on a keypad to disengage the alarm system that was beeping steadily. As soon as he had finished, the tiny red alarm light changed to green and the alarm was silent.

In the large kitchen he switched on soft lighting that fell over whitewashed oak cabinets and a pale-yellow tiled counter. Jason caught Meredith's wrist lightly. "Come here," he said, leading her to the sink. She wore black boots and black, lumpy sweats that hid her figure. And he knew from falling on her and pinning her down in the car that she definitely had a figure. Pulling out a towel, he ran warm water over it and then turned to scrub her face.

"I'd like to see what you look like. You've been a dark blob from the first moment I saw you," he said, looking down at her as he tilted up her chin. At the sight of her in the light, he drew a sharp breath and remorse filled him because she had a raw scrape on her cheek and he knew he had caused it. When he touched her jaw lightly, she jerked her head away.

"I'm sorry you're hurt. I thought you were a boy."

Thickly-lashed, large, stormy gray eyes gazed up at him, and the moment his gaze met hers he received the second stunning blow from her. Her eyes took his breath and held him mesmerized. He couldn't recall ever seeing eyes exactly the color of hers. But it was something more than color that held him breathless. He felt as if he had touched a live wire and sparks were flying all around him. Silence stretched; he realized she was as still as he and he didn't want to break the contact.

She took the cloth from his hand and began to rub black off her face. He retrieved it, wanting to touch her, wildly curious now to see what she looked like without all the junk on her face. And still neither one of them had spoken or moved or looked away.

"We need to clean up your scrapes quickly. Just a minute and I'll be back.'' Silently, he called himself all sorts of names for causing her face to be scraped raw as he hurried to the nearest bathroom. He returned with a bottle of peroxide. "Lean over the sink and let me pour this over your cheek. It'll clean your scrape and disinfect it. How long since you had a tetanus shot?"

"Only a year ago."

She tilted her head and he poured the clear liquid, dabbing gently. "Sorry, if I hurt you."

"Oh, yeah, sure," she grumbled, and he felt worse than before. Finally he patted her cheek dry. "Let's see your hands."

"I can take care of my hands."

"Put your hands out and let me help," he ordered. When she held them over the sink, palms up, he winced, hating that he was at fault for her injuries. He washed the scrapes, cleaning and disinfecting them. "I wouldn't bandage those scrapes tonight. Maybe tomorrow when you'll be out in the world, but let them heal tonight. Now, let's get off the rest of whatever you have smeared on you." In slow deliberate strokes he wiped her face gently, while he continued to look into her eyes. The longer he rubbed her face, the faster his pulse beat.

Finally, he had to rinse the cloth because it was covered in whatever she had spread over her face. In silence he rinsed it and returned to a task that was ever so pleasant, slowly stroking her face free of smudges. Besides the fabulous eyes, she had a slightly upturned nose, full pouty lips and prominent cheekbones.

She yanked the cloth from his hand. "I can wash my own face," she snapped and turned to wash over the kitchen sink. She slanted him a look. "If you'll tell me where the bathroom is, I'll wash in there."

"You're fine where you are," he said, not giving a rip about the sink and interested in the smooth, rosy skin beginning to show.

As she shook water off her hands, he handed her a clean

towel, and she scrubbed with it vigorously, something he had never once seen a woman do.

Big gray eyes peeped at him over the towel, and he wondered if he should get ready to dodge her fist again, but she merely folded the towel.

Reaching out, he pulled the cap off her head. When long, slightly curly auburn locks spilled out, he drew a swift breath. Unruly, silken strands curled around her face. From what little he already knew, she was fiery, impetuous and fearless.

"You want anything to eat or drink?"

"No, thank you," she replied with disdain.

"Come here," he said, taking her wrist again and leading her through the kitchen, down the hall, into the spacious family room. He led her to a wide, brown leather couch that faced a large brick hearth. With a little tug he got her to sit down and he faced her, releasing her wrist. "Now, why were you slashing Dorian's tires? What's going on between the two of you?"

Two

Meredith Silver thrust out her chin stubbornly. "I don't have to answer any of your questions," she snapped. No man should look so sinfully handsome. He had black curly hair that he wore long, and it gave him a wild, dangerous look. His features were slightly rugged with a strong jaw, prominent cheekbones and straight nose. It was his thick lashes and blue-green eyes that had stopped her in her tracks in the kitchen.

Meredith wished she hadn't stood there like a starstruck teen looking at a movie idol, because she suspected Jason Windover drew women the way flowers drew bees.

She glanced beyond him to study the windows. This was no fortress, although he had turned off an alarm system when they entered. She knew how to hot-wire a car, and later tonight she was getting out of this house and away from this man who was becoming a big interference in her life.

"I can still call the sheriff and have you locked up. This

is a small town and most of us know each other pretty well. He can come up with some charges to hold you in a cell for a while.''

Her mind raced. She knew lawyers because she had solved computer problems for various ones, but not recently and she had never made lasting friendships with any of them. She didn't know a single lawyer to call for help. Besides, compelling bedroom eyes were staring at her, an invisible push to get her talking.

''I've been trying to find Dorian Brady. Now I've found him and he's telling everyone that I'm crazy and that everything I'm saying about him is a lie.''

''Well, is it or not?''

''I'm telling the truth, but he's your friend and your good-ol'-boy fellow club member. Y'all are a bunch of snooty male chauvinists, and I know you'll believe him over me, so what's the point in even discussing this with you?'' she said, becoming more annoyed as she talked because a twinkle had come into his eyes.

''What's the point in slashing his tires?''

''I just want him to know that I'm here. That I'm in his life and I'm not going to go away. I want to cause that man some grief.''

''He knows you're in his life, and you are causing him a little grief. But I'll tell you what, all those good-ol'-boy male chauvinists have voted that I'm to keep you out of everybody else's hair, so that's just what I'm going to do. Tonight, you can just stay here under my roof until you simmer down. And tomorrow you can go back to wherever you came from.''

''That's what you think, mister.''

''Jason is the name, remember?''

''Mister is sufficient. We're not going to be friends.''

''Now that's another challenge you've just flung at me,'' he drawled, and she definitely saw the twinkle in his eyes that time.

Thrusting out her jaw, she leaned closer to him. "I will never be friends with a man like you, buster!"

He looked as if he was making an effort not to laugh out loud. He leaned close. "Why not, Meredith?"

Oh, my! She was going to have to watch it around this one. He was sexy and too handsome and his voice sent shivers skittering around inside her. And those bedroom eyes of his! She moved back and drew herself up. "I'm sure most women just melt when you bat your eyes at them, but I'm not melting, nor will I. I—"

"Challenge number three," he stated, this time speaking in a slow drawl and looking at her with a speculative gleam in his eyes that made her draw a swift breath.

"I'm not flinging sexy challenges at you. I'm telling you. You probably can't believe that a female in this whole big state of Texas is immune to your charm."

"Darlin'," he drawled in a tone that did curl her toes and sent a flash of heat that threatened to melt her, "I haven't even begun to turn on any charm. Knocking the wind out of me doesn't exactly draw out the best aspects of my personality."

"You attacked me."

"I stopped a vandal from escaping," he reminded her. He took her wrist again. His brows arched. "Your pulse is racing, Meredith."

She glared at him while crimson flooded her cheeks. "Don't flatter yourself. It's fright."

"You—*afraid?*"

"There's good reason to be," she snapped, pointing at her scraped face and annoyed that her pulse was reacting to him in a wild, uncontrollable manner.

"I'm sorry I hurt you," he said, and to her surprise, he sounded truly contrite. "Come on. Let's get something to drink. I definitely want a drink."

"I'll come without you holding my hand," she said, attempting to yank free.

"I think I want to keep one hand under control. You

have a wicked punch there. Besides, I don't want you heaving one of the family heirlooms at me and breaking some favorite vase."

"I wouldn't think of it."

"Not much you wouldn't."

He was tall, broad-shouldered and a very sexy male. Having him hold her wrist made her nervous, even though his grip was light. When she had tried to get free, he had held her without effort, but she knew that wasn't what bothered her. It was the physical contact with him, however slight, that set her pulse racing.

Maybe if she humored him until he locked her in a room—and she was certain that's exactly what he would do sooner or later—then she could try to escape. Once they were in the kitchen, he released her wrist. While he pulled a cold beer out of the refrigerator, Meredith studied the windows and latches, which looked quite ordinary. And she had watched when he had turned off his alarm, so she could remember the series of numbers he had punched in. She was certain Jason wouldn't think she'd try to escape, especially since they were so far from town. He had left his pickup near the back door and if she could get outside to his pickup, she would be on her way.

"Want some pop?"

"I am not drinking or eating with you."

"Suit yourself," he said, and turned to open the bottle of beer. They returned to the sofa where he sat too close for comfort. She could detect his aftershave, see the faint dark stubble on his jaw.

He set his beer on a coaster on the large cherrywood table standing in front of the sofa. He pulled off a boot and set it aside and then pulled off the other one. "We might as well get comfortable."

She was half tempted to say she wanted to go to jail, but his house was cozy and there weren't any bars on the windows and she stood a far better chance of escaping from this ornery Texan than she would from a jail.

"Now tell me why you want to cause Dorian grief."

"He's a wicked man. But I know you don't believe a word I'm saying because he's in your good-ol'-boy group."

"Let me decide that."

"One of my sisters was engaged to him."

"He denies that. Do you have any proof?"

"Proof of their engagement? No, I don't."

"Did he give her a ring?"

"He told her that he was having his grandmother's diamond ring reset. He kept putting off why it wasn't ready and at the time, he sounded convincing. He can be charming and he's good-looking and he's clever. Everything sounded logical, so I didn't doubt what my sister was telling me. Twice I had dinner with them, and I had him at our house," she said. As Merry talked, she had to constantly gaze into those sexy eyes and she could hear how lame her story sounded. There wasn't a flicker of emotion in Jason's expression, so she had no idea what he was thinking.

"*Our* house? Are you married?"

"No, I'm not. I live in an apartment in Dallas, but I go home often to the house where I grew up. My mom is a Dallas news anchor and I grew up in Dallas."

"Another well-known family member." He tilted his head to study her. "Your mom isn't Serena Dunstan, is she?"

"Yes, she is. Her real name is Therese Silver, but Serena Dunstan is her professional name. How did you guess?"

"She's the right age and she's done some controversial reporting—and won awards. Hank Silver, Serena Dunstan—you're from a whole family of feisty daredevils."

"My sister Holly isn't. She's a little on the shy side."

"I would have to see it to believe it," he remarked dryly.

"Mom's certainly more well-known than my brother. I'm really close to my three younger sisters, so I'm at our house most of the time. My youngest sister, Claudia, is in high school now, but she graduates this spring."

"I hope she's not the one Dorian was supposedly engaged to."

"It isn't supposedly," Merry said darkly, knowing he was friends with the creep and wasn't going to believe a word she said. "Dorian was engaged to Holly, who finished college early and has a great job as an engineer."

"Do you have pictures of them together?"

"No, I don't," Merry answered flatly, realizing how flimsy her accusations were beginning to sound up against Jason's practical questions. "There was always a reason why Dorian did or did not do something. When I wanted to take their pictures, he'd put me off and then we'd forget all about it." The more she talked, the more her anger built again. "I thought Dorian just decided all of a sudden to dump her, but now that you're asking all these questions—reasonable questions—he must have planned to do this from the very start. She really was in love with him," Merry said, remembering Holly sobbing and shaking and refusing to eat far too many times. For the past few months she had watched her sister lose weight steadily.

"Holly believed Dorian and was taken in by him. She had bought a wedding dress—"

"No ring, but she bought a dress?" Jason asked doubtfully, as if Holly were lost in fantasies.

"I can't tell you how believable he made it all sound."

While blue-green eyes studied her, she wondered what was running through the lanky Texan's mind.

"Men can be very convincing when they want to. Even in the biggest of lies," she added.

A shuttered look altered Jason's expression slightly. "I don't think you should limit that to men," he said in a cynical tone that surprised her.

"I can't believe any woman ever hurt you. I'll bet you draw them like flies to honey."

The twinkle returned to his eyes. "Whatever makes you think that?" he asked with great innocence.

"Stop fishing for compliments! You know you're a good-looking and sexy stud."

"Son-of-a-gun, darlin'," he drawled. "You will turn my head. So you think I'm a sexy stud?" The words rolled out like soft velvet sliding across her skin, and Meredith wished she hadn't said anything. When would she learn just to keep quiet? But then, how could she sit in silence when he was looking at her with an eagle-eyed intentness that made her nervous and made her want to chatter?

"Why don't we go out to dinner tomorrow night? I can drive to Dallas," he said.

"Thank you, but I have other plans. And I'm not leaving Royal."

"You have friends here in Royal?"

"No, I don't know anyone except Dorian, and now you. I'm staying right here in Royal. You can't make me leave town."

"You plan to slash Dorian's tires again?"

"No, I won't," she said, annoyed with him and trying to ignore the little nagging voice inside that wanted to accept his offer of a dinner date. "I wouldn't tell you anyway, but I don't have other plans. I just don't care to go to dinner."

He grinned, a full-fledged, heart-stopping grin with perfect white teeth, and she tried to catch her breath and not stare. With an effort she shifted her gaze to her fingers laced together in her lap. She had just turned down a date with that grin. Just sitting there doing nothing, the man was handsome, but when he smiled, he was to-die-for gorgeous. His smile could melt the coldest heart. She just knew it had better not melt hers. And she knew he had an ulterior motive in asking her to dinner because he was trying every which way to learn her plans about Dorian and to keep her away from him.

"I'm sure you're unaccustomed to any female turning down an offer of a date with you, but I'm not interested."

"Well, in that case, we'll sit right here at my house. You

can go with me tomorrow to pick out a computer and we'll have dinner at home and you can help me set up a new computer—''

"You're kidnapping me!"

"No, I'm not. You're free to go. You want to leave, I'll take you straight to the sheriff. After all, I caught you in a criminal act."

She glared at him. "I don't want to go to jail. I'll think about it tomorrow."

"I wouldn't want to go to jail, either. My house is far more comfortable, and I'm better company that any of those deputies and you can have something to eat or drink whenever you want." He gave her a speculative look. "You know, men have been breaking women's hearts and vice-versa since the beginning of time. Your sister got jilted by a low-down lying rascal—as you would say—but that happens. When it does, you pick up and go on with life."

She bristled. "How easy that is for you to say! You're a playboy and I'm sure you're incredibly experienced at breaking hearts. I'll bet you've left a path strewn with them back to when you were just out of elementary school."

"Grade school? I don't think so!" he said and rewarded her with another fabulous grin.

"And I'll bet no female has ever broken your heart. So don't even talk to me about how unimportant a broken heart is!"

He tilted his head. "Another swift punch—somewhat undeserved, I think. I've always made it clear that I'm not a marrying man. I'm not into commitment and I always state that up front. I have never been engaged to anyone and never hinted at engagement. So don't lump me in with broken promises of engagement. There's a difference. Anyone who dates me knows exactly how I feel about marriage. I'm very open about it. Most of the women I date feel just the way I do."

"Why aren't you a marrying man, if I may ask?"

Again, she caught that brief shuttered look and a muscle

working in his jaw. He had some touchy point, something that had happened to him that had soured him on marriage.

"My brothers have had disastrous marriages that have torn apart their lives and hurt their children. I don't ever want to go through that."

She suspected there was more to the story than he was telling her, but they were little more than strangers and she could understand why he would be reluctant to tell her about himself. As he talked, he unbuttoned his shirt and rolled up his sleeves. She didn't think he was aware of what he was doing, but she was certainly aware of the slight glimpse of a tanned, well-sculpted chest.

"Those sweats may be rather warm for this time of year. Want something more comfortable?"

"That would be nice," she said and he stood, reaching down to take her wrist.

"You don't have to hold me."

"Only your wrist. I can keep up with you better this way," he answered lightly, but it made her stand closer to him than was comfortable. He had to be a couple of inches over six feet tall. The top of her head reached his shoulder and she felt as if tiny currents of electricity were jabbing her when she was close to him. The prickly awareness put her on edge because it was so uncustomary for her. What was it about him that caused the sparks? Surely not just his movie-star looks. She shouldn't be susceptible to bedroom eyes and a high-wattage grin. Something about him had her heart skipping way too fast and she could just imagine the broken hearts he had in his past.

They entered a large hallway decorated with Western art and he directed her back across the kitchen to another hallway. "The east wing of the house has spare bedrooms, my office and a workout room. We don't use these bedrooms unless everyone is home."

"Who is everyone?"

"My brothers and their families. They've remarried and have kids. We spend a lot of time here," he said switching on lights and she entered another large, comfortable room with leather-upholstered furniture. A pool table was in the center of the room with a Ping-Pong table in a far corner and an immense stone fireplace along one wall. A wide-screen television stood at one end and one wall was lined with shelves filled with books. Two large gun racks were against another wall with an antique sword mounted over the fireplace.

"I can see why. You have everything you need here at home."

"Not quite," he drawled, and she knew he was referring to a woman companion.

"Don't you get lonesome here?" The moment she asked, she knew it was a ridiculous question, and she answered before he could. "I know you don't get lonesome anywhere. I'm sure I'm keeping you from some woman's company tonight, and I'll bet she's quite unhappy about it."

"No, I told you. There's no one in my life right now."

"If there's not, she must be only a day away. I can't imagine you going ten minutes without a woman close at hand."

"Tonight I've got you, darlin'," he drawled lightly, and she knew he was teasing her.

"And I know full well you didn't want me."

"I didn't say that. I'm just assigned to keep you out of trouble."

"To keep me away from Dorian is the truth. You can't watch me forever."

"Nope, I surely can't, but for tonight I can do my assignment."

She was acutely aware of his fingers still circling her wrist. Moving close at her side, he led her to another large room where he switched on a light. "Here's my office."

"What a beautiful desk." When she wriggled her arm, he released her. As soon as he did, she crossed the room to look closer at the satinwood-and-ebony desk. "This looks old."

"It is. My grandfather brought it home from Europe on one of his travels. I've tried to add some antiques to this home since I've had the house."

"This is a beautiful desk," she said, running her fingers along the smooth wood. Antique glass-fronted cases held books, but before she could read the titles, he took her arm lightly and led her back through the kitchen toward the center of the house and the west wing. "We'll be staying in this end of the house."

While they sauntered down the hall, Meredith considered escape. Maybe if he drank a few more beers, he would sleep dead to the world and her escape would be even easier.

"I'm surprised you don't keep a dog out here."

"There are several dogs on the ranch, but they're down at the bunkhouse with the men."

"Don't tell me dogs don't like you."

He glanced at her with amusement in his eyes again. "I get along fine with the dogs. They're just shut in the bunkhouse at the moment. Want me to get one of them up here?"

"Heavens, no! I just found it unusual to be out in the country and not see a dog."

"Well, city girl, the dogs are here. I'll show you tomorrow. Right now, I'll show you around the house. Here's the dining room."

She looked at a large room with a Texas-size carved, mahogany table that held ten chairs on each side and two arm chairs at each end. A sparkling crystal chandelier caught the light and silver gleamed on the buffet. Another brick fireplace was at one end of the room.

"Do you actually eat in here?"

"Sure. The table is over one hundred years old and my great-great-grandfather had ten kids. The Windover descendants are all over Texas. We have big family get-togethers, and each of my brothers has four kids, so that's at least twelve people when they come home. There's a guest cottage in back for the overflow."

"What about your parents?"

Again she caught the briefest shuttered look before he turned his head away and switched off the dining-room light. They moved down the hall. "My parents were divorced. I haven't seen my mother since childhood, and my dad died last year."

"I'm sorry you lost your father. My dad died when I was eleven."

"I miss my dad," he said gruffly. "Eleven must have been a rough age to lose your father."

"It was, but my parents were always very involved with each other and not as much with us kids. Particularly my mom. My mother was just not meant to be a mother. I was always mother to my sisters and that was all right with me and good for Mom. Dad helped with the girls."

"So you were mother to your sisters. Was your brother Hank the second dad?"

"Hardly," she answered dryly. "Hank's wild. When Dad died, Hank got more wild. He's in trouble half the time and he's out of touch with the family. I haven't seen him in over a year."

"I sort of remember that he'd been in some scrapes," Jason said politely, and she could imagine that if he knew her brother, he knew some of the predicaments Hank had been in.

"If you know Hank, you must ride in rodeos."

"I used to, but I haven't had time in the past few years. I was a saddle bronc rider. I did a few months of bull-riding, broke my arm and quit."

"I don't know how many bones Hank has broken."

"Here's the living room," Jason said, switching lights on in a formal room that was exquisitely furnished and looked as if no one ever used it, much less a houseful of men. It was the one room that did not appear to hold any antique furniture, and it struck a slightly strange note with the rest of the house.

"This is a nice room," she said, noticing that the blue satin drapes were faded, but still looked elegant.

"Yeah, well, we don't spend time in here," he said, switching off the lights. His voice was harsh, and she realized there were undercurrents in his family that he didn't talk about. She suspected he didn't talk about a lot of the facets of his life. She was beginning to decide the real Jason Windover might be hidden from the world.

"Here are the bedrooms," he said, switching on lights and moving down the hall as she looked into rooms that were spacious, masculine and comfortably furnished. "My bedroom is the master bedroom at the end of the hall and I'm going to put you in here tonight, right next to me, so I can hear you."

He switched on a light and crossed to the closet. She looked at an elaborate Louis XVI bed of dark, hand-carved mahogany. A tall chiffonier matched the bed. The room had pale-green and off-white colors, and, as she looked around, she wondered how many other women had stayed in it.

He tossed out a cotton robe. "Here's a robe. I'll give you some of my T-shirts so you can get into something cooler. There's the bathroom and towels are in the cabinet. Change and we'll get something to eat."

She nodded and he motioned to her. "First, come see my bedroom, and I'll give you the T-shirts."

She followed him to a spacious bedroom with a brick fireplace, shelves of books, another large television, a tall, rosewood armoire with an ornate cheval glass beside it. A second keypad for the alarm system was in his room, so he could switch it on or off from either end of the house. A king-size four-poster bed dominated one end of the room and a stack of books stood on a table beside the bed. She strolled over to see what he read and looked at titles about the Second World War.

"You like history."

"Yes," he answered while he rummaged in a drawer and handed her a stack of folded T-shirts. "My grandfather was in the landing at Normandy in the Second World War. He kept a diary of sorts and because of that, I got particularly interested in that war."

Jason thrust the pile of shirts into her hands.

"Thanks. I'll need only one."

"Take them all. After we say good-night, don't try to leave the house. I have the alarm turned on. If you open a door or a window, it will trigger the alarm. When we go to bed, I'll change the setting and the alarm will go off if you step into the hall. You're in a cell here. It's just much nicer than the one in Royal."

She nodded again, left his room and went to hers, closing the door behind her. She showered and washed her hair. She found a dryer and dried her hair. It had a natural curl and was unruly, but tonight she didn't care. She pulled on a navy T-shirt and slipped back into her sweatpants and then left to find him, returning to an empty family room and then going to the kitchen where he was making sandwiches.

He glanced over his shoulder and then turned to look more carefully at her, and she wished she were back in the lumpy sweatshirt. The T-shirt clung, and the look he was giving her was making her tingle all over.

"My goodness, Meredith, you clean up good."

"My friends call me Merry," she said breathlessly, knowing she needed to re-engage her brain. The man was definitely *not* one of her friends. Nor would he ever be one.

He crossed the room to her, stopping only inches away, and she hoped he couldn't hear her drumming heartbeat.

"So we're going to be friends," he drawled in that deep, sexy voice. He reached out to touch her hair, letting locks slide through his fingers, and she was aware of the faint contact. "That's interesting."

"I spoke before I thought," she admitted.

"You don't want to be friends?"

"I don't think it's possible."

He focused on her face, moved closer and tilted up her chin. She was too aware of his finger holding her chin, too aware of all of him. "I am sorry about your scraped cheek and hands. You shouldn't ever have something like that happen. I hate that I caused your scrapes and bruises. I'm sorry."

"You should be," she said, wishing he would move away, but unable to move herself. Another one of his riveting looks nailed her and she gazed back, too aware of the silence stretching between them. "You're standing too close," she said, aware she was hemmed in by him and the kitchen cabinets behind her.

"I am? I disturb you?"

"You're not adding me to your list of broken hearts, Jason, so just move back and give me room."

"All those challenges," he said quietly without moving an inch, placing his hands on the cabinets on both sides of her and moving even closer. "Now do you really expect me to ignore them?" he asked softly. "You're the one who brought them up."

"I didn't mean any of them as challenges to you. I'm not impressed. I'm not interested. I don't want to go to dinner or anything else with you."

"You might hurt my feelings."

"There's no way I can do that," she said, finding every word more difficult to get out. He stood entirely too close and he was entirely too handsome. And she was being far less than truthful when she told him she wasn't impressed. Oh, my. She'd bet the house that his kisses would melt any recipient into a bubbling blob.

"I have a heart that can be broken just like anyone else's."

"I think your heart is locked away behind impervious armor and no woman will ever get to touch it."

He ran his finger along her throat, a faint touch that sizzled. "I'm not invincible."

"I don't care to find out. I think you said we were going to drink something," she reminded him, trying to look away and glancing first at his mouth, fleetingly wondering what it would be like to kiss him. Why would she wonder something like that about a man like Jason Windover? Had her brain gone completely to mush?

"Oh, sure," he answered as if that were the last thing on his mind. "What would you like?"

"Just some pop."

He moved away, and she could breathe again. Watching him as he walked around the kitchen, she was thankful his attention had shifted from her. He brought her pop poured over ice in a tall glass, and he carried another beer and she hoped it would knock him out for the night, yet he had a way of slowly sipping them that made them last.

Finally they were settled back on the sofa in the family room. Jason sat too close with one arm stretched on the back of the sofa and one leg bent, his knee on the sofa only inches from her thigh. He offered her a sandwich which she declined. He helped himself.

"I think you should forget about Dorian and go home," he said, taking a bite of his cheese sandwich.

"Maybe so."

"You don't mean that. You're just patronizing me until I'm out of your sight. You can't change him. You can't accomplish anything. You're just a fly buzzing around his head annoying him."

"Maybe that's all, but he deserves to be annoyed."

"Merry, I said it before and I'll say it again. Women have jilted men and broken their hearts. Men have jilted women and broken their hearts. When it isn't a deep commitment, you just pick up and get over it."

"I'm sure that's the philosophy of your life," she said, becoming aggravated with him again. "My sister is losing weight. She's broken-hearted. Her work is getting neglected. Her life is suffering.''

"She's got to get over him. Introduce her to new guys,'' he said, finishing his sandwich and taking a sip of beer.

"She doesn't want to meet any guy right now.''

"I'll repeat, when there hasn't been too deep and too lasting a commitment, then broken hearts mend.''

"Thanks, Abby, for that bulletin.''

"It's the truth. They weren't married. They hadn't known each other for years.''

"That's so easy for you to say! She's heartbroken and I want him to know he can't walk all over someone and then turn his back and walk away. I want to cause him some grief. He's hurt her and taken her money—''

Jason turned to look at her. "Dorian took money?''

"Yes. Holly didn't have a lot, but she's very thrifty. She has a good job and she's saved quite a bit for having just been out of a college a few years.''

"Are you certain he took her money?''

"Now you're interested,'' Merry said, once again annoyed with him. "Money's important to you, but Holly's broken heart isn't.''

"There's a difference. If he took money, he may have broken the law,'' Jason said quietly, and she realized she had his undivided attention now.

"Tell me exactly what Dorian did,'' Jason said.

Three

A broken heart was one thing—but missing money was quite another. All of Jason's cold, negative feelings about Dorian returned. Suppose he had been right about the man all along? Money was missing at Wescott Oil and some of it had turned up in an account in Sebastian's name. Someone had taken that money and tried to frame Sebastian for murder. A man had been killed, and the guilty party was a cold-blooded murderer.

Jason realized Merry was studying him intently. "What?" he asked.

"What's going through your mind? Dorian taking Holly's money disturbed you."

"We've had something going on here in Royal," he said, choosing his words carefully. "You've met some of the Texas Cattleman's Club members," he remarked dryly, and she did have the grace to blush.

"I just wanted to find out where Dorian was. I'm sure it

was a dreadful shock to have a woman violate the inner sanctum of your precious club."

"You weren't exactly quiet about it," he said, thinking that was all he'd heard about the day after Merry had burst into the club demanding to know Dorian's whereabouts. Merry was a fiery, feisty, Texas tornado, stirring people up everywhere she went. Was she that way at home in Dallas? He found it difficult to keep his mind on the conversation, on Dorian, on problems, when she was sitting close and looking so enticing.

Since her shower, Merry's hair was silky, springing free to curl slightly around her face and spill onto her shoulders. Its deep auburn color held highlights of gold and fiery orange. In the kitchen he had wanted to kiss her. And he had almost tried because he thought she wanted him to, but the moment had passed. Now he wanted to stretch his arm out about three more inches and touch her. He resisted the urge, focusing on their discussion.

"Do you remember meeting Sebastian Wescott?" he asked.

"Dorian's half brother. I thought he was nicer than Dorian."

"Ahh, we agree on something," Jason said, having resisted touching Merry as long as he could. He wound locks of her hair around his fingers, letting her soft curls slide over his hand. There was a flicker in her smokey eyes and pink tinged her cheeks, so she had noticed and she wasn't objecting. Was the lady feeling the same sparks that he was?

"Sebastian inherited the Wescott Oil empire and when Dorian arrived in Royal and let his presence be known and that he was a long-lost half brother, Sebastian took him in and got him a job at Wescott Oil in computer services."

"Sebastian Wescott should know that he has taken in someone who is deceptive and unscrupulous. Dorian is a real snake."

"We've inducted Dorian into the Texas Cattleman's

Club because he's Sebastian's half brother. He seems to have fit himself into life in Royal.'' Only half thinking about Dorian and Sebastian, Jason talked while his thoughts were on Merry, her big eyes, her soft hair that he was winding around his fingers. She sounded sincerely annoyed with him. His usual ability to charm a woman seemed to be failing. But, he reminded himself, they hadn't gotten off to the best of starts. Still, for whatever reason, he wasn't accustomed to women disliking him and it bothered him. It also bothered him greatly that he was the cause of her skinned cheek. Her skin was as soft as a rose petal and he wished he could undo the harm he had done.

"And—"

He realized he had stopped talking as he studied Merry and wondered about her.

"Sorry. My mind wandered. Where was I?"

Her brows arched while her gaze filled with curiosity. "Where did your mind wander?" she asked softly.

His pulse jumped. "To you. What you're like, your soft hair—"

"Your attention better wander back to Dorian Brady."

"That's not nearly as much fun."

"It's safer."

"Scared, Merry?"

She gave him a sultry look that sent his temperature soaring. "Not at all. I'm not your type, so let's get back to facts. What were we talking about, Rob Cole?"

"Don't be in such a rush to change the subject, now that it's on us."

"There is no 'us.' Tell me about Rob."

He was tempted to keep flirting with her, but good sense took over, and he knew she was right.

"Rob Cole's wife, Rebecca," Jason continued, trying to disengage himself from a spell that Merry seemed to weave effortlessly, "found the body of Eric Chambers, a man who worked at Wescott Oil and was murdered."

"How awful!"

"Eric had been strangled. Eric was Vice President of Accounting at Wescott. Money was missing at the company. When some of it was found in a private account of Sebastian's, he was arrested and accused of the murder. There was a very incriminating e-mail that Sebastian supposedly sent to Eric."

"That sounds terrible," Merry said. "At the trial Sebastian must have walked, or I wouldn't have met him at the club." She shook her head, causing the locks wound in Jason's fingers to slip free and he wondered if it really bothered her that he was touching her hair. The last thing he ever intended to do was force even the slightest unwanted attention on a woman. Yet, when they had locked gazes, Merry had been as immobile as he. And in the kitchen when he had moved close, she had been breathless. Just minutes ago, she had flirted with him. Curious about his effect on her, he ran his finger across her knuckles while he watched her face.

When he saw the faint flicker in her eyes, his pulse jumped. Maybe his attention wasn't unwanted after all.

He took her hand in his gently, careful not to touch her scraped skin. "You have small, delicate hands, Merry."

She yanked her hand away and balled it into a fist in her lap. "What happened after Sebastian was arrested?"

"The case was dismissed. He had an alibi that he couldn't talk about, but his attorney found a way to prove that he couldn't have committed the murder, so someone was obviously trying to frame him. Someone planted evidence in Sebastian's office that indicated he was responsible for the missing money."

"That's dreadful!"

"Dorian might stand to gain a lot if Sebastian were out of the way. It's one thing for a man to break your sister's heart. It's another to cross the line and steal her money."

"The money isn't as important as deceiving her."

"Maybe not, but it tells me more about Dorian's character."

"It doesn't say one thing more about him than what I'm telling you that he did in deceiving Holly."

"All anyone knows about Dorian's past is what he's told us," he said. "Tell me about the money."

"All right. Holly let Dorian talk her into opening a joint account. He said that when they married everything would be jointly shared anyway. He told her he didn't believe in keeping things separate. What was his was hers and vice versa. So she did."

As Merry talked, Jason watched her. If he had good sense, he wouldn't flirt with her or touch her. This was definitely not a woman he wanted to date. Not in the next million years. And yet—what was it about her that drew him? A few casual touches shouldn't hurt anything. She was going to ignore them anyway.

"By your standards I'm sure she didn't have a lot," Merry continued. "Holly worked hard and went without things and saved. She had several thousand dollars, and he just cleaned it all out and was gone."

"That's an entirely different matter than running out after telling a woman he loved her."

"It's different if you think money is more important than love!" she snapped indignantly and he knew he had just lowered himself in her sight again, but he was lower than a snake already so another notch wouldn't matter.

"Do you have records of this joint account and of the withdrawal?"

She flushed again, and he wondered whether she was making everything up. "Dorian kept the records. He told Holly that he was moving the account to a bank where they would get better service. She gave him all the receipts. I don't have proof of anything he did. He was very clever." Big eyes stared at him. "You don't believe me, do you?" she asked, sounding resigned as well as aggravated.

He thought before he answered. "I sort of believe you, but I sure as hell wish you had proof. Do you know how much better it would be if you could pull out bank statements, that sort of thing?"

"He took the money," she said stubbornly. "And I'll bet he's tied in with whatever is going on at Wescott Oil. The man is greedy, ruthless and totally unscrupulous."

Jason stared at her while he mulled over his own negative feelings about Dorian. He shouldn't let them color his judgment now, though.

"I'm not convincing you," she said and she sounded discouraged and resigned.

"I'm listening and thinking about it, but proof would make a world of difference. You know the old saying about a woman scorned."

She stood. "I'm exhausted and I'd like to go to bed."

"Sure." He came to his feet. "In the morning do you want to sleep in or do you want me to call you?"

"I would much rather sleep in."

"Suits me fine," he said, thinking of appointments he would have to juggle to stay home with her. Yet the thought wasn't unpleasant. "I'll be up early. I work out first thing. You may use my exercise room if you want."

"Thanks. I usually work out in the morning, too."

"I'm not surprised at that," he remarked dryly.

Switching off lights, he walked down the hall with her. He glanced at her out of the corner of his eye. He had rarely dated short women and hated to have to stoop down to kiss one. It was much more pleasant to have an armful of tall, soft woman than to have to bend himself into a pretzel shape to get a hug and a kiss. "Are you between jobs right now?"

"That's right."

"So you can take time to get out and slash tires and break into men's private clubs and all that?"

Her eyes narrowed and she shot him a look that should have dealt as big a blow as her fist, but he wasn't one to be intimidated by looks.

"Dorian Brady is evil, and I don't think he should do his wicked deeds and not have some comeuppance."

"Maybe you should let the law worry about comeuppance."

At the door of her bedroom, she turned to face him. "You can't keep me here indefinitely."

"I don't intend to. I got you off the street tonight and as long as you leave Dorian alone, you can go your own way. Will you leave the man alone?"

She seemed lost in thought. "I suppose," she said with a sigh.

"I think he's suffered."

"You are birds of a feather," she remarked darkly.

"I told you before that I've never promised a woman marriage, never taken a dime of a woman's money. Please do not lump me with Dorian Brady," Jason said, annoyed with her again. She was like eating hot peppers—tasty, but full of sting.

"All right. I apologize for lumping you with him," she said.

"Thank you." He placed his hand above her head, resting his palm against the jamb. Moving closer, he tilted her chin up. "You know, the night doesn't have to be wasted."

"Wasted?" she asked, sounding breathless. He slipped his hand to her throat and discovered her racing pulse. He wasn't waiting for her arguments or protests that he was sure would be coming. Pretzel twist or not, he wanted to kiss her. He slipped his arm around her waist, stepped closer and leaned down.

The moment Jason's arm went around her waist, Merry opened her mouth to protest, but his lips covered hers and it was as if she had stepped into space and was into a dizzying free fall—and on fire at the same time. When his tongue touched hers, her heart thudded. His tongue slipped across hers, stroking and exploring her mouth, melting her into a trembling mass of breathless woman.

Mouths together, tongues together, bodies together. She

couldn't resist him even though she knew she should. His kiss was dynamite with a million tiny explosions, yet beneath the fireworks, something seemed great.

Standing on tiptoe, she slipped her arm around his neck and held him. Lordy, the man was tall. And breathtaking and a heartbreaker. A world-class heartbreaker who always let women know they wouldn't be permanent fixtures in his life.

Clinging to him, she trembled, kissing him eagerly in return as his kiss became more demanding and passionate. She was lost in it, drowning in heady sensations. This couldn't be happening, but it was. It was all too real, all too intense, making her want so much she knew she could never have. Where were her wits?

She stopped kissing him back, pushed against his chest and then was standing facing him once again. The moment she pushed, he moved away.

There had never been a kiss like his. Not once in her lifetime, and she was shaken badly. She wasn't widely experienced with men, but she suspected if she had been widely experienced, she still would have had the same reaction to Jason. Breathing hard, he looked down at her.

Words failed her, and she simply entered the bedroom and closed the door in his face.

Then she felt idiotic. She should have said something and not acted like a kid with a first kiss. But it was too late to open the door and start a conversation now.

Dazed and flustered, she stared at the closed door. No wonder he left hearts broken everywhere. It wasn't fair. He was too handsome, had a smile that would melt a glacier and had kisses that could seduce the coldest and wisest heart.

She moved to a rocker and sat down, staring into space. Closing her eyes, she remembered his kiss. He probably hadn't even enjoyed kissing her. Goodness knows, he had stopped fast enough! *Oh, my*. What a kiss! She had turned down a dinner date with him. She wanted to jump up, run to his bedroom and tell him yes, she'd go to dinner with him. Except she couldn't. She didn't want to be just another one of his conquests, and she suspected if the number of them were known, it would be a Guinness record. Maybe not that many. He seemed sort of a nice guy. Her lips still tingled, and she had other things to think about, but for the next hour, she was just going to sit here and remember the best kiss of her life.

An hour later the house was quiet and dark. Her eyes had adjusted to the darkness and she had rummaged around and found little things she thought she might use: a paper clip she straightened, a nail file. She dressed in her dark sweats again with a cap on and she opened the door of her bedroom and lay down on the floor. Carefully, taking time, she slithered into the hall. The alarm system would either be one of those heat-sensor ones or it wouldn't. If it was a garden-variety motion detector, it might not pick up movement very low to the floor.

Expecting the siren to scream at any second, she inched her way, moving her arm so carefully and then the other arm. Next she slid her body, trying to stay pressed as close against the floor as possible and to move as slowly as possible. Her ears felt as if they were growing as she strained for the slightest sound.

She was thankful his hall floor wasn't carpeted. Instead, he had a plank floor that made it easy for her to slide along. With her body weight spread, there were no creaking boards either. Pray the man slept soundly and for hours longer!

If the alarm went off, she was going to make a run for it, but after covering five yards and no alarm, she thought maybe she would make it all the way to the back door and the alarm keypad.

Sleep, sleep, she silently urged Jason. Perspiration poured off her face and she was on fire in the hot sweats and clinging cap. It seemed hours and miles to the back door.

When she reached the back entryway, she wondered how long it had taken her. She was afraid the sun would be coming over the horizon. As a rancher, he probably rose before the sun, so she wanted to be out of the house as soon as possible. She wiped perspiration from her face on the sleeve of her shirt. She was hot, miserable and tense.

She neared the keypad. If the alarm system was typical and this door was keyed in as the entry door, she would have some thirty seconds to turn it off before the alarm would go off. But with her first movement, it would begin emitting tiny beeps that might wake him. She thought about the numbers she had watched him punch. If she got them wrong, all her effort would be for nothing and he would be after her and catch her before she could reach his pickup. The man was a very fast runner.

Taking a deep breath, she stood and swiftly punched the combination of numbers she had watched him use. As her fingers flew over the keypad, there were four tiny beeps from the alarm, and she prayed he slept soundly.

Without looking back, she unlocked and opened the door. As soon as it opened, it set off another three small beeps, but no loud alarm went off when she stepped into the cool night. Taking a deep gulp of air and half expecting him to clamp a hand on her shoulder or tackle her again, she raced to his truck. Thank Brother Hank for teaching her how to hot-wire a car.

Seconds later, the motor roared to life, and she grinned. "Whoo hoo!" she yelled when she put the pickup in gear. "So long, cowboy. You'll get your pickup back later today!"

She floored the accelerator, skidded and settled to a speed that stirred up a plume of dust as she laughed triumphantly and raced away from Jason's house.

While she drove into town, she planned her next move—another little annoying reminder to Dorian Brady that he had not gotten away with his schemes without any reprisals.

Sometime soon, she intended to confront Dorian about

Holly's broken heart, but she knew he would just deny that he knew anything about Holly and say that he had never been engaged.

Her smile of triumph over escape vanished as she thought about Dorian and Sebastian and all Jason had told her about Wescott Oil. Could Dorian be behind a murder and the attempted effort to frame Sebastian Wescott?

Feeling chilled, Merry realized she might be dealing with a very dangerous man. If he was involved in murder, then his dirty dealings went far beyond lying to Holly and stealing Holly's money and trying to frame Sebastian. Holly was fortunate the man was out of her life. Merry hoped the day would come when Holly would see that.

The more Merry thought about Dorian and Wescott Oil, the more certain she became that Dorian had to be the murderer. No one would believe her, though. She didn't have one degree of proof; just because he had deceived Holly and taken her money, that didn't make him a murderer. Merry wished now she had asked Jason more questions about the murder.

When she reached town, the eastern sky had the faintest gray tinge. She parked the pickup in front of the Royal sheriff's office. That way, if Jason reported it stolen, they would find it quickly. She climbed out, locked the pickup and walked swiftly down Main Street to the Royalton Hotel where she left word at the desk that under no circumstances was she to be disturbed. So much for Mr. Jason Windover.

In the dark of his bedroom Jason slept, dreaming an erotic fantasy about Merry Silver until dreams spun into empty reality. In the dim recesses of waking he was aware of a motor. And then he was fully awake.

For a full two seconds he stared into darkness while he listened to the roar of a motor that was rapidly fading away. Then Jason lunged out of bed because he recognized the sound of his own pickup.

He didn't think it was one of the hands leaving in the

dead of night, and none of them would have taken his pickup without asking. Jason yanked on briefs, glanced at the house alarm and stopped in his tracks as he stared at the steady green light that meant the alarm was turned off.

"What the hell?" he asked no one. He ran, yanking open the door to the bedroom next to his and staring at the neatly made empty bed. He raced down the hall in his briefs, plunging through the back door and outside to stare at where his pickup had been parked. A cloud of dust still hung over the road.

"How the hell did she get out?" he snarled, running his hand through his hair. "Dammit, wildcat."

She couldn't be far down the road. As he hurried inside and returned to his room to yank on his jeans, he mulled over his choices. He could turn in his pickup as stolen and have her thrown in jail. He could go after her, but she had a head start and he suspected she would drive fast.

"Dammit," he swore again. The woman was more trouble than a basket filled with snakes. She might not even return to Royal. She might be headed to Dallas. He didn't think she would keep his pickup, though, and she had a car somewhere in Royal, he was certain.

He yanked on a T-shirt, pulled on his boots and began to stuff his pockets with his wallet and keys. He could drive the car into town. He didn't know how she had managed to get to his keypad to turn off the alarm without setting it off, but he realized that when they'd arrived at the ranch, he had been careless in turning off the alarm. He hadn't tried to hide the code from her because he didn't think she was paying attention anyway. And he hadn't thought she would have any chance to use the code.

What was one of the first things he had been taught? Don't underestimate the enemy. Well, he had grossly underestimated this little enemy. Damn, she was trouble! She wasn't doing anything except annoying Dorian and the rest of the club members. Jason grimaced. She was annoying the hell out of him. He remembered kissing her. He didn't want to remember because her kiss had all but melted his teeth. Her kiss had gone deeper than just hot—stirring some feeling that was totally foreign to him. He had to get her out of Royal and out of his hair.

He locked up and jogged to the garage, swearing under his breath. Here he was in the dead of night, his pickup stolen, outsmarted by a five-foot bit of trouble—that was embarrassing. He thought of the foreign assignments he'd had, the assignments with the Texas Cattleman's Club. He had been up against the toughest of the tough and here this little five-foot wildcat had outwitted him—his own damn fault for underestimating her.

He should have slapped handcuffs on her and made her spend the whole night beside him. And then he *really* wouldn't have gotten any sleep. He didn't want to think about her kisses or her body or those great big smokey eyes or her soft lips that set him on fire. He was not going to think about any of that. He backed out of the garage, turned the car and raced up the road for the highway, trying to shake thoughts out of his mind that he didn't want there.

He should just call the sheriff and turn her in and let her rot in a jail cell. It would serve her right. He thought about her silky skin that was raw and skinned because he had tackled her and he knew he couldn't have her arrested and thrown in jail.

"You're getting soft, Windover," he told himself. The hell he was. He was getting hard just thinking about her and her delicious mouth. He swore and pressed the accelerator and wondered what she would do next.

As he cruised Main Street, he spotted his pickup. In spite of his aggravation, he had to grin because she had parked it squarely in the sheriff's reserved parking spot.

Watching for her, Jason cruised down Main until he reached the Royalton. He turned into the lot and let a valet have the keys. Inside the quiet hotel with its potted palms, plush oriental carpets and high ceilings, Jason strolled to the desk, his pulse jumping with satisfaction when he recognized the stocky blond clerk behind the desk.

"Morning, Mr. Windover."

"Hi, Stan. I didn't know you worked here."

"Yes, sir. I've been here almost a year now."

"Do you like it?"

"Yes, sir."

"Stan, what room is Meredith Silver in? I need to talk to her."

Stan frowned and looked uncomfortable. "She said no one was to disturb her. I'm sorry."

"All I want to do is talk. You know I wouldn't harm a woman."

"Oh, no, sir!"

Jason pulled out his wallet, withdrew a fifty-dollar bill and carefully folded it and slid it across the counter. "Just tell me the room number. I'm not asking for a key. I just want to slip a note under her door or talk to her if she will talk."

"Mr. Windover, gee." The fifty had already disappeared into Stan Fogarty's hand. "It's room three-one-seven. But I didn't tell you."

"Thanks, Stan. She won't ever know that you told me. I promise, no trouble."

"I hope not, sir."

Jason crossed the lobby, entered the hall and took the stairs. In minutes he was in front of her room. He pulled a small wire from his pocket, picked the lock and quietly turned the knob.

The room was dark and he slid inside, closing the door behind him without a sound. Ready to get revenge, he switched on the light.

Jason blinked and stared at the smoothly made bed. He spun around, looking into the bathroom, the closet, the rest of the room. There was no luggage, nothing. Had she gone back to Dallas? In the early hours of the morning? Where was she? And had she given up pestering Dorian? She hadn't checked out or Stan would have told him. She had left orders not to be disturbed. He had a gut feeling the woman was still right in Royal, but if so, where was she?

Jason knew that he had underestimated her at every turn and it was beginning to annoy him. He better start thinking that he was up against a very intelligent operative instead of five feet of aggravating fluff. He circled the room again. He could smell her perfume. He glanced in the bathroom. A wet cloth hung over a rack. She had been in here, but was gone.

Feeling ridiculous, he looked under the bed and searched the closet that held nothing except extra pillows and an ironing board. Finally, he switched off the light and went downstairs.

"Stan, has Miss Silver checked out?"

"No, sir. She just said she didn't want to be disturbed."

"Well, I didn't disturb her, so you can relax. Tell you what," he said, pulling out a ten-dollar bill. "If you see her again," Jason scribbled on a piece of paper and handed it with the ten to the clerk, "will you call me on my cell phone?"

"Sure. You don't have to give me any more money."

"Keep it. Thanks for your help."

"Yes, sir, Mr. Windover. Anytime."

Jason walked out and waited to get his car. When the valet brought it and stepped out, holding open the door, Jason noticed a small square of white paper fluttering beneath the windshield wiper. It was not the time of night or day for anyone to be advertising or selling something. And he hadn't been parked illegally. He pulled out the note and looked at the neat printing. "Your pickup is in front of the jail. Thanks for the loan of it."

He wanted to kick a tire, but he had the disgusting feeling she was somewhere watching him and laughing and he didn't want to give her the satisfaction. He swore quietly and steadily, every word in his native tongue and a few in other languages that he knew.

"Sir, is something wrong?" the valet asked.

"Sorry, no." He tipped the man and climbed into his car, then looked up at the Royalton. Every window was either dark or if a light burned, the drapes were pulled. He couldn't spot anyone looking out a window, but he couldn't see them all from inside the car. He hit the steering wheel with the palm of his hand. "Dammit!" Where was the wildcat? And what would she do next?

Four

Filled with reluctance, later that morning Jason strode into the quiet, elegant meeting room at the Texas Cattleman's Club. Coffee was served in the tall silver samovar on a sterling silver tray. Thin-bone china cups edged in gold with the club crest were beside the silver service.

Within a few minutes all eyes were on him as Sebastian stated, "Dorian's tire was slashed. We assume you apprehended Meredith Silver after that. Now, have you sent her back to wherever she came from or is she still out at your ranch?"

While the question hung in the air, Jason could feel his face flush. He rubbed his fingers along the soft denim covering his bent knee. "She's not at my ranch."

"So?" Rob coaxed. "Where is she?"

Jason faced ten pairs of curious eyes. "I don't know where the hell she is," he grumbled, and Rob let out a whoop.

"Could it be a woman has gotten the best of our resident playboy?"

"Dammit—" Jason started, but then they were all laughing.

"Our CIA agent has been given the slip by a slip of a girl—" Sebastian said, grinning.

"By a little wildcat," Jason remarked, knowing he would have to endure their teasing. "I sort of underestimated her. I'll find her—"

"How long ago did you 'lose' her?" Rob asked, grinning broadly.

"I'll find her soon enough."

"Find her before she does some other damn mischief. I had to buy a new tire," Dorian snapped, looking less than amused, but the others were still laughing.

"You may have to go back to the CIA for a little more training on how to secure and hold your prisoner," Rob needled, still chuckling.

"When did you last see her?" Sebastian asked with a twinkle in his eyes.

"Last night she was at my ranch—"

"She got away from you at your ranch?" Rob asked incredulously. "How'd she do that? I thought you had an alarm system."

"I do—"

More laughter drowned out his statement, and Jason grinned. "I'll find the wildcat today," he assured them.

Rob's smile faded. Looking relaxed, he sat back in his leather chair, but Jason noticed that Rob was intently studying each man. "On a serious note, there's something we have to discuss. We're trying to discover what we can about Eric's murder. Sebastian has been cleared of the charges against him, but there is still a murderer loose in Royal. And for reasons I don't want to go into right now, it looks as if there may be a mole in our organization." The words wiped all amusement off every face and felt like an icy wind sweeping through the room. A chill ran down Jason's spine as he instantly thought of Dorian, but kept his attention on Rob who continued to gaze solemnly at each of them in turn.

"How can we discover who it is?" Keith Owens asked, his brown-eyed gaze circling the room.

"I suppose all suspicion lands immediately on me," Dorian announced. "The rest of you have known each other for a lifetime and now this crazy woman is accusing me of things I haven't done."

"No one is making any accusations at this point," Rob said. "We just need to be more alert."

They continued discussing the problems at Wescott Oil, but the conversation wasn't as free as before, Jason noted and the group soon broke up with suggestions on how to catch his quarry and more good-natured teasing. Before they disbanded, he managed to ask Rob to wait a few minutes.

As soon as they were the only two left in the room, Jason closed the door. "I want to tell you what I learned from Merry."

Rob burst out laughing again. "How'd she get past your alarm?"

"It's a thousand years old, and I'm having a new one installed today. Dad put that other one in when I was a kid."

"You didn't take her car keys?"

"Shut up, Rob, and let me tell you something."

Grinning, Rob nodded. "Go ahead."

"She told me about Dorian jilting her sister."

"Which he denies. Is there any proof?"

"Not a shred. She said that he always had reasons for what he did or did not do. He avoided leaving any incriminating trail: no pictures, no ring, nothing. She'd bought a wedding dress and was planning her wedding when he left. He cleaned out her account."

Rob's brows arched. "Any proof of that?"

"No, but I wanted you to know what Merry said."

"Merry? You're on a first-name basis. That's good."

"I'm telling you, shut up."

Rob laughed and then sobered. "Do you believe Meredith Silver? Slashing Dorian's tires and bursting into the club doesn't give her much credibility."

Jason remembered big smokey eyes, her earnest voice. "I think she's telling the truth."

"We'll keep an eye on Dorian. In spite of his rock-solid alibi, it's beginning to sound suspiciously as though he's our man. And if he is, I don't need to tell you, he's dangerous." Rob clamped a hand on Jason's shoulder. "There's a good rookie cop I can get when he's off duty to help you keep an eye on the Valkyrie."

"Go to hell, Cole. I'll find her today." Jason snapped, knowing he would be in for teasing for the next few weeks, if not longer.

The two men walked out together and parted in the parking lot. As soon as he slid behind the wheel, Jason turned the ignition, driving out of the lot and heading for the Royalton Hotel. He was going to find Merry Silver and when he did, she wasn't getting away again.

Two hours later, as he sat in a hot car across from the Royalton, he swore under his breath. "Where is she?" he asked himself, climbing out of the car and deciding to take another approach to locating Merry.

Merry spent the morning looking at apartments, finally deciding on one a block off Main Street. She met the landlord at the office, a tall, gaunt man named Willard Smythe who was unhappy to discover she didn't have a regular job. For once in her life, Merry tossed out a mention of her mother's vocation and as she expected, she won Mr. Smythe's grudging approval.

He reminded her of a crane, with his long legs and tufts of blond hair and a peculiar way of jutting his head out, and she suspected he would have liked to turn her away.

"This is a very quiet area, Miss Silver," he stated firmly.

"I lead a very quiet life," she said, or she had until Jason Windover had crashed into it.

"Hmpf. Most of our tenants are widowed or married. We don't have young singles. Now on Berry Street there are two apartment complexes you might find more to your liking."

"I like this place. It's quiet and charming. May I see the apartment that's available?"

He sighed and stood. "Come this way." He stopped at the door to look at her. "Miss Silver. Let me repeat—this is a very quiet place. There are no wild parties."

Since when did she look like the wild-party type? she wondered. "I promise that you'll never know I'm here except when I pay my rent."

"Yes. Well, we'll hope," he muttered and turned to lead the way to a small apartment that faced the front gates.

The two-year-old apartment had lots of glass that gave it a sunny, spacious look even though it was small. The entryway opened onto a living area, an adjoining small dining room, a kitchen that was bright and cheerful in blue and white. She liked the cozy, high-walled patio, although she didn't expect to have the apartment for a long time.

The security of twenty-four-hour armed guards at the gates was reassuring. After cajoling, holding firm and finally making a deal with Mr. Smythe to help him get his records into computer files, she made arrangements to rent the apartment for a month. She made a deposit and drove back to the Royalton, circling the block and spotting Jason's black pickup parked along the curb across from the hotel.

Jason wasn't in the pickup, but she couldn't be certain he wasn't close by, watching for her, so she kept driving, circling around and approaching the hotel from the back entrance. She turned into the hotel parking, gave the valet the car key and entered the hotel, stepping into a gift shop to survey what she could of the hall and lobby. She didn't

see a tall Texan, a broad-brimmed hat or any other sign of
Jason.

Moving carefully to the stairs, she hurried up and in
minutes closed the door behind her as she entered the second room she had rented at the hotel. It was expensive to
have two rooms, but it had enabled her to escape being
found by Jason last night. This room was rented under her
youngest sister's name: Claudia Barclay. Claudia Barclay
Silver had an old family name as her middle name and it
was serving Merry well now. She didn't want Jason to find
her again soon, so extra precautions were in order. She
didn't think he believed one word of what she had told him
about Dorian Brady.

"Men!" she said aloud. She set down the bag of items
she had in her arms and began to plan for the evening.

That night Merry sat in a corner booth in the almost
empty Royal Diner. Only one waitress was working and
Manny was cooking. The short time she had been in Royal,
Merry had heard about Manny's hamburgers and his pork
chops. She had also heard about Jason Windover's playboy
reputation.

Through the window of the grill kitchen Manny was vis-
ible in a white undershirt that revealed muscled shoulders
and arms. At the long Formica countertop, red, vinyl-
covered bar stools stood empty which was a relief to Merry
because a crowd would interfere with her plans. An old
sentimental ballad played on the ancient jukebox.

Excitement bubbled in her because she was going to
strike again in Dorian Brady's world. And she was exu-
berant because the entire day she had eluded Jason Windover. At various times she had seen him watching the
hotel. She was tempted to leave another note on his pickup,
but by doing so, she might be pushing her luck.

Almost an hour ago, she had ordered a burger and fries
and pop and had a book propped in front of her so it looked
as if she were reading while she ate. No one seemed inter-

ested in her, and she surreptitiously watched the single waitress and now the only other customer at the diner, Dorian Brady, who sat three booths away from her. The whole time he had been there he had flirted with the waitress and the woman was constantly at his table, hovering over him and giggling at things he told her. Merry caught the name Laura.

Dressed in navy slacks and a blue sport shirt, Dorian looked handsome, yet Merry could only feel anger every time she looked at him. She wished she could warn the waitress, who seemed as taken with him as Holly had been.

Merry touched the blond wig she wore and adjusted the fake glasses on her nose. When he'd entered the restaurant, Dorian had glanced her way, but he had never looked at her again. And he shouldn't recognize her even though he knew she was in town. The blue sweats she wore were well padded, adding lots of pounds to her appearance.

Motioning to the waitress, Merry asked for her check and in minutes the woman brought it to her.

As soon as the waitress left, Merry pulled a cellular phone from her pocket. It was nine o'clock and dark outside. Dorian should be just into the first few bites of his dinner. Merry had seen them bring him chicken-fried steak, which suited her purposes fine. She placed a call, turning her back on the room.

"Royal Diner," the waitress answered.

Merry whispered, "Tell Dorian Brady he better check on his car." She broke the connection quickly and slipped her phone into a pocket.

As the waitress hurried to Dorian's table, Merry slid out of the booth to cross the diner to the cash register to pay her bill. She heard the brass bell over the door jingle and glanced around to see Dorian leaving.

"Was everything all right?" the waitress asked as she stepped behind the register to take Merry's cash.

"It was fine," Merry said.

"Good. Thanks for eating here. Come back again."

"Sure. Thanks," Merry said. She collected her change, walked back to her table and left a tip. Then she strolled toward the door, looking at the empty diner and the waitress with her back turned while she brewed a fresh pot of coffee. Manny was bent over with his head in a refrigerator.

Merry passed Dorian's plate and paused to shake the contents of an envelope over the thick gravy covering his chicken-fried steak. With one more glance at Manny and the waitress, Merry picked up Dorian's fork. Ignoring her pounding heart, she stirred the gravy and then replaced the fork and strolled out into the cool night. Heading back into the diner, Dorian passed her, but he didn't glance her way.

She climbed into her car and left. "Now, Mr. Dorian Brady, see how you like that!" she said. Soon the man would realize that his misdeeds wouldn't go completely unpunished.

She returned the back way to the hotel, took the stairs and whipped out her key. She would stay in her room tomorrow and maybe venture out the next day.

She stepped into her darkened room, heaving a huge sigh of relief as she reached for the switch. The light came on and her heart lurched.

"Howdy," drawled Jason, who sat with his long jeans-clad legs stretched out in front of him.

In shock, she stood immobilized. "How'd you get in here?" she asked in stunned amazement that he had found her.

"It wasn't difficult. Now that's an interesting outfit."

She began to pull her wits together and come out of her shock. All she wanted to do was get away from him.

She spun around, grabbing the door and yanking it open. With her heart pounding, she ran.

Hearing him behind her, she headed for the stairs.

An arm snaked around her waist, and she was yanked back against a rock-hard, lean body. He tossed her over his shoulder again and strode back to her room, kicking the door closed and locking it.

Crossing the room to the bed, he dumped her on it un-ceremoniously and stepped to one side, out of kicking range.

"You're not going anywhere without me."

She was breathing hard, angry and still shocked that he had found her. There was no way to be forceful with the man when she was flat on her back and he was standing over her. She struggled to her feet.

"This is my room and you get out."

"You have the same choice tonight you had last night. You're coming with me or you're going to jail. And judging from the way you're dressed," he drawled, studying her as if she were a bug under a microscope, "you've been up to something."

Her heart lurched again. She didn't want to go to jail. She didn't want Jason around when the news came out about Dorian.

"Call the sheriff. I'm not going with you anywhere," she snapped, trying to give herself a minute to think and to get out from under Jason's blue-green gaze.

"Suit yourself," Jason drawled and strolled to the telephone, punching the number for an outside line, then punching more numbers.

"Is Sheriff Escobar in?" he asked.

Merry's heart thudded as she dashed across the room and broke the connection. Better Jason Windover's ranch than a cell. And she didn't want to be sitting in jail when they got word about Dorian eating a dinner laced with chili peppers.

"I'll go to your ranch."

"Fine." he said, replacing the receiver. He stood too close and his gaze was too intense.

He touched her blond wig. "This is interesting," he said, carefully removing her wig and tossing it on a desk. He removed the fake glasses. "Blond wig, fake glasses, makeup that isn't like you at all." He ran his fingers through her hair and tingles shot through her in the wake of his strokes.

"And this," he said, holding her shoulders and stepping back to look her over. His finger punched her waist, but she felt nothing because he was poking the padding she was wearing.

"My, my. No one would look twice at you, would they? It's a pretty good disguise. Did it work?"

"I don't have to answer you."

"No, you don't. You've been up to something. You've done something to Dorian. Am I going to read about it in the papers?"

As her cheeks burned, she moved away from him.

"Pack your stuff. You're moving to my ranch."

Glaring at him, she watched him move to the chair and sit down as if he had no cares in the world. How could the man look so relaxed and then move so fast?

"I want to shower."

"Go right ahead. I'm in no hurry. There aren't any windows in the bathroom and the air vent is too tiny for even you to wiggle through."

She gave him another glare and began gathering up her things.

"If I am going to read about Dorian in the paper—or worse—hear about him on the late television news, you might be better off to tell me."

"I don't have one thing to tell you."

He shrugged, and she continued gathering her clothes, too aware of flimsy lace underwear in her fist. She hurried to the bathroom and locked the door, thankful to escape his watchful eyes. How had he found her?

Annoyed and worried, she showered, washed her hair and took her time. She dressed in jeans and a blue T-shirt and when she finally emerged from the bathroom, he was reading a magazine.

Her suitcase lay open on a bed. Wordlessly, she flung her things into it as he watched every move she made.

"I had a new alarm installed today. You won't get past this one."

"I didn't intend to," she answered as haughtily as she could.

Amusement flared in his eyes while he came to his feet. "Ready to check out of both rooms? You won't be needing them."

"I think I will just go home to Dallas. You can follow me."

"No way, lady. Today you rented one of the most exclusive apartments in Royal."

"How did you find out—" She clamped her mouth shut, determined she wouldn't give him the satisfaction of knowing how shocked she was that he already knew about the apartment. The man wasn't as out of it as she had first thought. She couldn't guess how he had learned about the apartment because she knew he hadn't been following her. If he had, he would never had let her get near Dorian tonight.

"Do you want to call home and tell anyone where you'll be? A boyfriend? Your sister? Your mother?"

"There is no boyfriend. I'll call my sister."

She called and got the answering machine. "Holly, I'll be at Jason Windover's ranch. The number is—" She handed him the phone and he said his number and gave her back the telephone.

"I'm fine and staying at the Windover Ranch. I'll let you know any developments." She broke the connection.

"Ready, Merry?" Jason asked.

When he said her name, another tingle slithered along her nerves. She nodded and headed for the door. He took her arm and she knew that, in the next few minutes, there wouldn't be any escaping him.

She checked out and they left. "What about my car? I can't leave it here."

"You won't have to. Give me the keys. I've already made arrangements to have the hotel keep it tonight and tomorrow one of my hands will pick it up and bring it out to the ranch.''

Silently she climbed into his pickup and sat far against the door while he drove.

"I'll say it again—you should let me know now if you've been out doing something evil to Dorian.''

"I don't have anything to say to you. You don't believe me about him, anyway.''

"I'm open-minded about it. It would be nice if you could come up with some proof, so keep thinking back. Seldom do people avoid leaving some kind of trail. Where did he work when he was dating your sister?''

"At Denworth Technology.''

"There, we can check on that.''

Merry watched Jason as he drove. His answer implied he was thinking about her accusations. "Tell me again about the murder,'' she said.

While Jason talked, she watched his hands resting on the steering wheel and then she looked at his handsome profile. The man was sinfully good-looking and she had to keep up her guard because she didn't want her heart to become another trophy.

"You're trying to find a murderer. I think it might be Dorian.''

Jason shot her a glance. "You don't like the man, but don't hang a murder charge on him when you have no proof.''

"You don't like him either, do you?'' she asked, feeling an undercurrent when Jason talked about Dorian. Jason's head whipped around in another swift glance.

"No, I don't,'' he admitted. "I don't have a reason either, which is bad. I usually like everyone I know. There's just something about him—I don't know what it is—''

"It's probably his insincerity. He's as phony as they come. Why don't you let me help on this murder investigation?''

Jason smiled. "You'll have to ask the police.''

"Cat's whiskers! You and those Cattleman's Club member friends of yours are investigating this, aren't you?" The idea just occurred to her and the more she thought about it and the little things he had said, the more certain she was.

"What gave you an idea like that?"

"You're not denying it, Jason. You know what I think—you said Sebastian had an alibi, but he couldn't tell people at first. That snooty club of yours is a front. You're involved in other things. Are you all a bunch of detectives?"

Silence stretched between them while he shot her another speculative glance. "No, we're not. That's rather perceptive, Merry. Rob is a private detective and most of us have military backgrounds with several of us having done some foreign work."

"I'm right, aren't I?"

"Look, most people don't know what we do. Let's leave it that way."

"I can keep my mouth shut."

"Then please do. It'll be safer for everyone concerned."

"I will, but not around you. You're not all detectives—so what's the deal?"

Again, he was silent a long time and she waited, watching him—which was oh, so easy—while he got an answer formed in his mind. At least he wasn't lying to her about it.

"We try to help people when they need help. We can go places and do things that officials can't always do. But that's strictly off the record and for your ears only."

She nodded. "I'll keep it to myself. It does raise my opinion of you somewhat."

He grinned that fabulous grin and shot her another quick look. "I thought I was right down there with the snakes in your book."

She had to smile in return. "Nope. Dorian's down with the snakes. You were a little higher in my esteem, but you've gone a little higher still since I know you are something besides a spoiled, rich playboy."

"Ouch! Look, I work. I hope I'm not spoiled—shoot, I might as well save my breath because I know I'm not changing your opinion." Another quick look shot her way. "I take it you're not exactly on poverty row since you booked two rooms at the Royalton and rented an apartment. You can choose your work assignments as you please."

She flushed and was glad it was dark inside the pickup so he couldn't see her. "I earn a living," she said.

"You graduated from college about five years ago?" he guessed.

"No. As a matter of fact, I enrolled at Texas University, went one year and landed a part-time job. Then I went home to a summer job that paid so much I never went back to college. But I'm going to get my degree," she said, fierce determination welling up in her. "I'm taking a correspondence course now. I'll get my degree."

"I'm sure you will if you put your mind to it."

"What did you major in?" she asked.

"Political science with a minor in animal husbandry."

"That's a weird combination."

"I needed both in my life."

They talked about college years and earlier until Jason turned the truck into his ranch. This time he parked in the garage, a distance from the house. When they entered his kitchen, he punched the alarm so swiftly, she wasn't certain of the numbers.

"It doesn't matter whether you got that combination or not—you won't slip past this one when it's set."

"I don't intend to try," she said, drawing herself up and receiving a disarming grin.

He reached out to brush her jaw lightly with his knuckles and she drew a deep breath. "I'm glad that scrape is healing."

"It's fine."

"We're not enemies?" he asked, his voice lowering a notch and a heated look warming his eyes.

"No," she said, aware he stood too close and she should move away, but she was rooted to the floor.

"Friends, then?" he asked, his hand stroking her throat.

"I suppose so," she whispered. Summoning all her will-power, she turned away from him. "Where do I put my things?"

"I'll put them." He picked up both suitcases and carried them to the bedroom that she had stayed in before. In a short time she was seated on his large leather sofa again, curled up in a corner and he was seated facing her only a little over a foot away.

"I've been thinking about all you told me. Did anyone question where Dorian was at the time of the murder?" she asked.

"He has an alibi—he was at the Royal Diner. Laura Edwards, a waitress there backed up his story."

"Another woman in love with Dorian."

"How do you know that?"

"You only have to look at the two of them together." Merry took a deep breath. "Why don't you let me help you catch Dorian?"

He gave her a smile that was as condescending as a pat on the head. "Thanks, but I don't think so."

"Why not? It looks to me as if you could use a little help."

"Your style is a little flamboyant. Right now he doesn't know he's under suspicion."

"It doesn't have to be flamboyant. I can be subtle."

"Thanks, anyway."

Jason was beginning to annoy her again. "If you can get me into Wescott Oil, I can get into Dorian's computer files."

Jason lowered his bottle of beer, set it back on the table and gazed at her patronizingly. "In a word—no. Thanks, anyway."

"You don't think I can do it," she challenged.

He shrugged broad shoulders. "No, I don't. You're into slashing tires and bursting into private clubs."

"I slipped out of here without your knowing it and got away with your pickup and eluded you all day."

"It was the luck of the amateur."

"Well, it sounds to me as if you guys are suffering the incompetence of the too-well-trained."

Amusement flashed in Jason's eyes while he shook his head. "Tomorrow I'll take you to town with me and buy a new computer. You can help me set it up here in my ranch office. I'll pay your going rate, of course. Okay?"

"Yes. Now back to Dorian. If you'll get me into Wescott, I can look at his files and I might learn something none of you know."

"You can't get into his files."

"Hah! It's an oil company."

"They have their computer people who are specialists."

"I can get into his files."

"You're mighty confident."

"I know my abilities and my limitations," Meredith said, hoping she could live up to her promises, but she thought she could.

The ring of the phone interrupted their conversation and Jason stretched out his long arm to pick up the receiver. He stood and turned his back to her, lowering his voice and moving a few feet away so she couldn't hear what he was saying.

He turned, glancing over his shoulder at her with a direct, annoyed look.

Dorian. Intuitively, she was certain the call was about Dorian. The man deserved a little upset in his life. If what she suspected were true about him, he deserved far worse than anything she had dealt him.

Jason replaced the receiver and turned to face her, his hands on his hips. "You're not accomplishing one thing except to aggravate Dorian."

She raised her chin and refused to bother defending herself.

"You put chili peppers in Dorian's dinner. What in blazes did you think that would do other than make him angry?"

"What makes you think I did any such thing?"

"Oh, come on—that was Keith, who was in the pharmacy when Dorian charged in. He was breaking out with hives because someone had laced his dinner with chili peppers. You're wasting your time, aggravating him and getting his guard up, and getting in the way of our investigation."

"So you *are* investigating what happened?"

"That's between you and me—if you can be trusted."

"You can trust me, but why don't you let me help you?"

"Why don't you stop doing these ridiculous things?" he shot back, sitting down again to face her. "You're not solving anything or helping your sister either."

His words stung because she knew he was right. Meredith wound her fingers together and looked at them. "I know you're right, but it was so terrible to watch Holly suffer and know that Dorian was getting off scot-free."

"Give it up and leave him to us," Jason said grimly.

"Maybe I'm going about this all wrong, but I didn't know Dorian might be involved in murder. I'll stop annoying him."

"Good. Do I have your promise?"

"Yes, but you should let me get to his computer. You're trying to catch a murderer here and whatever has happened is tied into Wescott Oil in some manner. Money was taken, a man was murdered. Let me look at Dorian's computer files."

"Dorian has an alibi. He couldn't have committed the murder."

"Yet you suspect him anyway."

"Yeah, maybe so. But breaking into his computer is illegal."

She gave him a look. "So is murder."

As Jason raked his fingers through his hair, Meredith watched dark locks spring back into place and remembered when she had touched the back of his head and his hair had curled over her hand.

He turned to stretch out his arm and snagged the phone again, placing a call.

"Sebastian, it's Jason. I've got Merry Silver here with me." He paused, listening. "That's right. I want to ask you something. Is there any way you can get us into Wescott Oil so she can look at Dorian's computer files?"

She waited, unable to fathom much from Jason's side of the conversation except that Sebastian was not enthused. Obviously, neither man believed she could get into Dorian's computer files and neither thought it worth the trouble to let her try.

Finally Jason replaced the receiver and turned to her. "How badly do you want to look at his files?"

"How badly do you want to catch him if he's the murderer?"

"Sebastian will help us, but he said there is no way he can get us into the building after-hours. We're on our own."

"What do you mean—'we're on our own'?"

"If you want into Dorian's office, we're going to have to break into Wescott Oil like burglars."

Five

"Why can't Sebastian just let us in?"

"He doesn't want to be seen with us. I don't blame him and I don't want him involved. Remember, he was recently arrested and I'm certain he's still being watched, so he shouldn't be seen with us."

"I understand."

"Up to a point, if we're caught, you've got a reputation in town for doing wild and crazy things, so I think we can talk our way out of trouble with the law. If a security guard finds you looking at Dorian's private files, that's another matter. And I don't want us to get caught. If Dorian has done what we suspect, we're crossing a dangerous man."

A chill raced down her spine as she thought about how much she had already antagonized Dorian. "So we're on our own."

"Basically. Sebastian will come out tomorrow and bring a map of the offices and building. He'll go over everything with us and he's going to unlock a back gate, but we have to get ourselves in and out of the building. Sebastian said you'll never get into the files. They have a highly sophisticated, hacker-proof system.''

Eagerness bubbled in her to get her fingers on Dorian's computer. ''I'll bet you a steak dinner that I get in.''

''Deal,'' he said, studying her. ''You're sure of yourself.''

''When it comes to computers.''

''I know computer types—you'll get engrossed in what you're doing and lose all sense of time. You can have twenty minutes to get into his files. If you can't access them during that time, we're getting out of there.''

''If we get past the guard, we should have plenty of time.''

''I don't want to take that chance. Twenty minutes. That's it.'' Jason lifted locks of her hair and curled them around his fingers. ''Still game?''

''Yes, I am. If Dorian's guilty of murder, I want him caught,'' she said forcefully.

''You have strong feelings, Merry.''

''I shouldn't have done what I did to him. It was foolish, but I hate how he hurt my little sister. I couldn't watch her suffer and not do anything.''

''You have to let go. She's all grown up now.''

''I know, but it's hard,'' she said, thinking of Holly. Jason pulled her into a gentle embrace and Merry looked up at him, relishing his arms around her, knowing he was right. She had to let go. Holly was a grown woman. As Merry gazed into Jason's eyes, all thoughts of Dorian or breaking into Wescott Oil fled.

What had been a comforting hug transformed. Sparks ignited, and her breath caught.

Jason's green eyes darkened, desire as easy to see as if he had spoken his feelings. Her pulse drummed. She wanted him desperately with a need she had never known before. This man was special, incredibly appealing no matter how dangerous he was to her well-being.

As he watched her, Jason wrapped his hand behind her

head and pulled her closer, leaning toward her while her heart jumped. Her hands went up to rest on his arms and then his mouth was on hers and he was kissing her.

Heat swept over her, and she leaned into him, kissing him in return while his strong arm banded her waist and he shifted her to his lap. His tongue stroked hers, and her roaring pulse shut out all other sounds. When her hand drifted to his chest, she felt his pounding heart. She wanted this tall, strong Texan, but she knew it was impossible and a threat to her future happiness. She would end up like her sister, with a broken heart and hopeless longings. Jason had made clear his feelings on commitment and Merry knew, even as she kissed him back passionately, that the only kind of relationship she wanted was one that would be permanent.

She pushed against Jason's chest and slipped off his lap. "Jason, you'll complicate my life, and we're not remotely compatible. You and I can't date each other."

"I don't know why not," he said gruffly, looking at her with so much scalding desire in his eyes that her will turned to slush.

"I want one thing. You want another. You don't want commitment. I do."

A shuttered look altered his expression, she could feel him withdrawing from her even though he hadn't moved a muscle. "Whatever you want, Merry," he said roughly. "I never go where I'm not wanted."

"I'm sure that's the truth," she stated, thinking it was a sin for him to be so handsome and charming when his attitude was so solitary.

"We'll talk tomorrow," she said, standing and leaving the room in a rush, afraid if she stayed any longer to talk, she would be right back in his lap.

The following night, butterflies danced in Merry's stomach as Jason slowed the truck behind the block that held the Wescott Oil building.

Landscaped grounds spread in front of the building and there were parking lots along one side and in the back. At the deserted side of the building, they stepped out of Jason's truck and crept to a locked chain-link gate. Jason reached through and carefully removed the partially open padlock.

Sebastian had said the back gate was rarely used and he would unfasten the padlock, certain the guard would merely give it a cursory glance when he did his rounds.

They slid through the gate, hurried to the dark shadows by the building and crept around to the front, which was well lit. They were both dressed in black. Merry's first glimpse of Jason in the dark shirt, black jeans and boots that emphasized his black hair, and made his blue-green eyes seem deep green had sent her heart hammering overtime.

In spite of the danger, it was difficult to keep her attention focused on their mission.

"You stay here," he directed, leaving Merry in the shadows near the front door.

Jason had purchased a cheap, noisy horn that he could easily activate. He had set it up with a battery operated timer, and she watched as he disappeared behind a car in the almost deserted lot. In minutes he came sprinting to join her.

"It should go off in one more minute. Your suggestion to put a couple of empty beer cans nearby should make the guard think kids were playing a prank. He'll have to get down on his knees to shut the thing off."

As Merry stood beside Jason, she could see the night guard sitting at the front desk, thumbing through a magazine.

While they waited, Jason stood close, his hand on her arm and she was only half aware of the danger of their situation, more aware of the danger to her heart from the cowboy at her side.

As they had made their plans, Merry had considered that these first few minutes would be their most vulnerable, and now her racing pulse could not slow.

Shattering the quiet night, the horn began a continuous, raucous blast. The security guard moved cautiously around the desk, paused at the door to peer outside and then stepped out. With his hand resting on his pistol, he crossed the parking lot. Moving cautiously he peered between the two cars and then disappeared as he knelt down.

"Let's go!" Merry said without waiting. Jason ran beside her and they made a stealthy dash, sliding through the front door and racing around a corner out of sight. At any second, she expected to hear a yell from the guard, but the only sound was their footfalls.

When Jason stopped abruptly, she bumped against him. He steadied her, pulling her close against his side as he pointed toward a door to the stairs. They moved more slowly, opening and closing the door without a sound. She was surprised how easily Jason managed all this—as if it were second nature to him.

They made the long climb to the executive floor, the tenth story of the building where the offices were spacious, elegant and locked. At the top floor she noticed Jason wasn't winded. He glanced at her. "You weren't kidding about working out. You just climbed ten flights without difficulty."

"So did you."

"I should have known from that first night," he remarked dryly and she grinned, remembering how she had caught him by surprise and knocked him flat. Her grin vanished as he hurried to a door and efficiently picked the lock.

In seconds he was through the outer door to the offices and then he was through Dorian's locked office door. Silent and dark, the empty office made Merry realize she was crossing a line now herself—taking risks to catch a criminal, but involving Jason, too.

He moved with the quiet certainty of a cat, and, again, she wondered about Jason's past. Then her thoughts shifted to the office and the task at hand. Walnut paneling, sheer drapes, oil paintings, crushed velvet upholstery surrounded a mammoth oak desk.

She studied Jason as he moved unhesitatingly to the desk and checked the drawers. "For a cowboy, you're very adept at breaking and entering."

She received another fabulous grin. "I retired recently from another job. I worked for the government," he said with a wink, and she realized how very little she knew about the man.

"Here's the computer," he announced, opening a cabinet and swiveling Dorian's chair around. "Do your thing. I'll stand guard. If I say someone's coming, you get out of here immediately. Just get out and get back to my car no matter where I am or what I'm doing. Agreed, Merry?"

"Yes," she answered, looking into his solemn gaze.

"Promise me."

"I promise. I don't know what you think I'll do."

"We don't have time for me to tell you."

She thought about the map that Sebastian had given them of all the offices on this floor. She knew the ninth floor held the accounting offices, but it was Dorian's office and computer that she was interested in. She had spent an hour late in the afternoon with Jason, both of them studying the Wescott Oil building map while she had been more aware of him than of the map.

Merry slid behind the desk and sat down, at home instantly when she was facing a computer. She switched on the CPU, watched the screen ask for a password and began to type.

She was unaware of Jason watching her or of him slipping out of the office and leaving her alone. The only light was from the screen, a bright glow that reflected on her hands as they moved on the keyboard.

Merry knew she had only a few tries to get this right.

It took her five minutes, but then the screen asking for a password disappeared and she was in. She scanned the menu and pulled up a file.

Merry lost track of time, but her pulse raced as she discovered that Dorian kept an electronic journal. She scanned it swiftly, her gaze skimming over words, searching for anything that might incriminate Dorian until the words: "...you don't want them to know..." jumped out at her.

The door opened and she looked around to see Jason. "Your twenty minutes are up."

"I'm in. Leave me alone."

She went back to what she was doing, unaware that he had closed the door and left. Slowing so her hands wouldn't shake, she inserted a floppy into the CPU and copied the file, skimming more lines while her pulse raced.

The moment she finished that file, she copied another one.

The door swung open and Jason thrust his head inside. "Someone's coming. Shut down!"

"One more—"

"You promised," he snapped, looking over his shoulder.

She clicked on another file from Eric Chambers to Dorian, hit Save and watched, standing while her pulse raced.

"Merry!"

She yanked out the disk and hit the close button.

"Stop what you're doing. I hear footsteps. Come on!" Jason urged, motioning to her. She dashed across the office.

"It isn't shut down."

"Don't care. Run!" Jason grabbed her hand and raced down the hall, still keeping sound to a minimum until they yanked open the door to the stairs and stepped inside. Jason closed the door silently behind him, and gasped, "We've got to get out of here."

While she clutched the floppy disk, they raced down the stairs. By the fourth floor the alarm had gone off, a high, ear-splitting shriek that turned her blood to ice.

"They know someone's in the building," Jason said. His hand tightened on hers and they moved even faster until Merry felt as though her feet weren't touching anything solid. The stairs seemed interminable, but finally they reached ground level. Releasing her hand, he sprinted ahead. They raced through the building, bursting through a back door. Now Jason wasn't making any effort to keep quiet. Alarms were blaring, all the lights on the grounds were on and she could hear sirens approaching.

"Suppose they shoot? We'll be easy targets."

He caught her hand. "If it's the Royal police, they'll fire a warning shot first. Then you stop running. Let's go."

She ran, aware that Jason was behind her. Was he trying to shield her in case anyone did open fire? she wondered.

They raced across the open parking lot, expecting at any moment to hear the guard charging after them, but they reached the gate without incident.

Gasping for breath, she yanked off the lock and rushed through to the truck, looking back to see Jason grab the padlock.

He stretched out his long legs, running to the truck to slide behind the wheel and they were off, spinning around a corner. In minutes they moved into traffic along Main Street. Jason had slowed to a sedate speed and her pounding heart was beginning to return to normal.

"We got away," he said at last. "Was it worth the risk?"

"I think it was," she said, holding up the disk. "There are things on here that I think incriminate him, but I'm not certain. I looked at everything so fast, it was almost a blur. I'm not certain I got the computer turned off. If I didn't, when Dorian comes to work later today, he'll know someone was in his office and into his computer."

"He'll know now. He was the one who came in."

"How on earth do you know that?"

"I heard him talking to the security guard as they were coming down the hall."

"Now Dorian will know someone was trying to get into his computer files," she said, chilled by the realization. "I backed out of his files. I just didn't get the computer off. He won't know for certain that someone got into them."

"He'll guess it was you."

"I suppose he will," she agreed.

"Don't try to get away from me now," Jason warned. "You may be in a lot of danger."

She shivered and locked her fingers together. "Now I'm glad Holly didn't marry him. When I can, I want to tell her all I've learned about him."

"Don't tell her yet because we don't know for certain. He knows you're at my ranch, but as long as I'm there with you, I don't think you're in danger."

"I could go back to Dallas."

"You stay right where you are," he said in a no-nonsense tone. He had been calm and in control through the entire episode while she was still shaking from their close call with security and with Dorian Brady. She took a few deep breaths and looked at the houses they were passing. She realized the foray was over. They had gotten into Wescott Oil, she had looked at Dorian's files, and she and Jason had escaped unscathed.

Fear changed to relief that was touched with jubilation. They had succeeded!

Impulsively, she turned and flung her arms around Jason and gave him a hug. "We did it! We got in and got out in one piece and I think I have something you can use."

"Hey!" he yelped, startled and glad they were on a deserted block at the edge of town and not speeding along the highway. He pulled the truck to the side of the street, turned to wrap his arms around her and hug her. Her face was inches away, and even in the dim lights on the dashboard, he could see the sparkle in her eyes. He wanted her and leaned forward to kiss her hungrily.

For one startled moment she was still and then her arms

tightened around him and she kissed him back, long slow kisses that made him forget they needed to get out of town, needed to avoid drawing attention to themselves, needed to resist touching and kissing and stirring up one iota more of the sparks between them.

She was fiery, wild and passionate and he wanted her with a need that shocked him. He wanted to shove her down on the car seat and take her right here, but for a dozen reasons he knew that was impossible.

As her tongue stroked his, Jason's senses were stormed. His pulse roared and he was hard, eager, ready. He wanted all of her and he was losing arguments with himself about holding himself in check. His hands slipped over her, following soft curves, resenting the jeans and shirt that were in his way. When he tugged her shirttail out of her jeans, she straightened, pushing against his chest.

Her breathing was as ragged as his. "We're in town and we should get out of here."

Jason couldn't answer. Fighting his urge to reach for her again took all his concentration. Yet he knew she was right, so he tried to get a grip on reason. He turned his attention to the road, glanced in the rearview mirror to see if they were being followed or if anyone had noticed them. Houses were dark, lawns undisturbed, the street deserted at this early-morning hour.

He put the car in gear and drove in silence, not trusting himself to speak, trying to get his thoughts away from Merry to something neutral, something that would take Merry Silver right out of his mind.

Chattering to him about the disk, she bubbled with excitement, yet he didn't hear a word of what she was saying. He wanted her desperately, and it took all his willpower to keep his attention on the road and head for home.

As they drove through the dark night Jason finally began to follow what she was saying and realized she thought she had something that could tie Dorian to the murder.

The moment they reached the ranch, she would want to look at the disk, he knew. That wasn't the urgent matter on his mind, but he was certain she was intent on discovering what she had copied from Dorian's files.

Jason turned onto his ranch road, and then he lowered the window and tossed out the padlock that he had removed from the back gate at Wescott Oil. It sailed high in the air and then dropped into a heavily wooded area with a tangle of underbrush. He had large uncleared areas on his ranch and few people ever bothered to explore them. He didn't want the police to speculate on why the padlock had been unfastened. Seb had enough problems to deal with.

The moment they entered the kitchen at the ranch, Merry waved the disk at him. "Can we look at this right now?"

"I kind of thought you'd want to," he drawled and they went to his office where she switched on the computer while he pulled a chair up beside her.

Jason watched her fingers fly over the keyboard and suspected she had already forgotten his presence. He openly studied her, knowing her attention was wholly elsewhere. He was curious about the files, but they were secondary to Merry herself. Since she had wrapped herself around him in the car, all he could think about was wanting her.

He ached to pull her into his arms, but he knew he should resist. Besides, he had a feeling he wouldn't be able to get her attention away from the computer right now. The damp night air had made her thick mane of hair curl more than usual and he touched her curls slightly. Just as he had expected, she didn't notice.

Leave her alone, he argued with himself. This was a woman who had told him she wanted commitment. He had no intention of having a long-term relationship with Merry or anyone else. Resist the lady, he reminded himself, yet still fingering locks of her hair in his hand and not wanting to break the physical contact with her.

He wanted Merry as he had wanted few women in his life and the thought scared him. He didn't want a broken heart—something he hadn't suffered for a long, long time. He didn't want to get hurt that way ever again.

"Look!" she whispered, and he tried to pull his attention from her to the screen.

He forced himself to read what she had on the screen, and then his attention focused on a daily journal by Dorian.

"I can't believe he kept records like this at the office," Jason said, looking at hints that Dorian was pleased with the way things were going and that he was getting money from Eric Chambers to keep something covered up. There were references to moving money and Jason whistled.

"There's not enough here to go to the police with, but it sounds to me as if Dorian was blackmailing Eric Chambers."

"I agree. Why would he keep this in his computer files?"

"He might not have had a chance at work to get them off his computer. With his alibi and the evidence pointing to Seb, there wasn't a reason for anyone to suspect him. And for a while after the murder, he might not have wanted to go to the office late at night to work because he might have been afraid of drawing attention to himself. He could have gone there tonight to get rid of his files," Jason said, knowing men often tripped themselves up, and Dorian was arrogant enough to think he could outsmart everyone.

"You can tell the two men knew about company money that was being shifted around, but there's no absolute proof that proves what was going on."

"You're right," he agreed, reading another file that she opened. In emphatic words, Dorian had told Eric to stop sending him messages with attachments, to get anything off his computer that they wouldn't want others to see.

"But there's enough here to point more suspicion at Dorian. A whole lot more suspicion," Jason said, too aware of the scent of her perfume as he moved closer to read the screen.

She tilted her head, studying Jason. "You said you used

to work for the government. You were at home with what we did tonight. What branch of the government were you with—Secret Service, Special Forces, CIA—what?"

"CIA."

She closed her eyes as if she had received a blow, and he wondered if, in her eyes, that was another mark against him. Smokey eyes studied him again. "Why did you quit?"

"I took a bullet in my side and spent some time in the hospital. It gave me time to think about what was important in my life. I took some time off and spent a few days in a little town on the coast of Spain. If the shot had been a few inches to my left, I wouldn't be here. I decided life is pretty good, and being a cowboy was a damned fine life."

"Why did you want to be in the CIA in the first place?" she asked, as if she couldn't imagine a single good reason.

"I got into the CIA because I wanted to do all I could for my country and I wanted the excitement. For a few years I had all that. Then home and ranch life and being a cowboy looked good again. Leave the wild stuff for the younger guys."

"You're *so* old," she teased.

"I'm twenty-eight now. There are younger guys who are eager and good at their jobs."

"I suppose your father was glad to see you come home."

"He didn't live long enough to know," Jason replied, gazing past her as if lost in his own thoughts. "My dad had a coronary occlusion and died suddenly while I was deciding whether to get out or not. He left the ranch to all three of us. I'm buying out my brothers' interests because they don't care about ranching."

Merry realized there were depths to Jason she hadn't guessed. His CIA background was sobering.

"Make about four copies of those files, will you?" As soon as she finished, Jason took two disks. "I want to get one of these to Rob tomorrow and one to Sheriff Escobar. Now, enough about Dorian Brady. Let's get a drink," he said gruffly.

They went to the kitchen where a low light burned over the sink. With deliberation Jason set the disks down on the counter. With every move his gaze was on her, and his eyes had darkened with desire. She was lost in his gaze, drowning in the longing in his expression, so intense it was doing things to her heart and other, more intimate parts of her.

He reached for her, his fingers closing on her slender arm. The moment he touched her, her heart thudded.

"Come here, Merry. I've waited all evening for this."

Six

His words echoed the silent message in his eyes and added to the heat and desire building in her. How could he do this to her with just words and a look? But he was. He was turning her inside out without so much as the brush of his fingers.

Merry knew he wanted to kiss her. She wanted him to, wanted to kiss him, wanted more of him than she could possibly have.

As he leaned down, he pulled her close against him. She tilted her face up, standing on tiptoe, closing her eyes. Heat flashed through her. Desire was scalding her skin while she tangled her fingers in his shaggy hair and kissed him. Instantly, his arms tightened around her, pulling her hard against his lean body. The taste of him, his touch, all his lean hardness was a wonder that shook her.

He picked her up in his strong arms, carrying her to the sofa and cradling her in his arms when he sat down. Why did she feel she had waited a lifetime for this moment? He held her in the crook of his arm while his other hand slipped beneath her T-shirt. When he touched her breast, she gasped with pleasure, lost in sensations so intense that the world vanished. Lights burst behind her eyelids and the roar of her pulse shut out all sounds.

She was barely aware when he released her to tug off his T-shirt, but then her hands were on his muscled, bare chest. She ran her fingers over scar tissue, realizing how close the wound had been to his heart.

"Jason," she whispered, knowing there was a chasm between this wild man who took risks and her very ordinary life. Yet differences couldn't stop her aching desire. He was hard against her softness. His body was warm, fascinating to her. She ran her fingers across his chest and heard him groan while he kissed her.

Jason swept her T-shirt over her head and tossed it away, his gaze searing as he unclasped her bra and pushed it aside to cup her breasts in his large hands. His warm hands were big, rough, tantalizing, his fingers driving her wild.

His callused thumbs stroked her nipples. Merry shook, wanting so much with him. She knew there had to be a stopping point, but not yet, ah, not yet. For a few delicious, stolen minutes, she was going to touch him and kiss him.

Then he leaned down to take her nipple in his mouth. His tongue stroked the taut peak, a velvety wetness that sent her into another dizzying spiral and she moaned softly, her fingers winding in his hair while her other hand played over his chest.

He was giving her pleasure, giving her memories, creating longings she hadn't expected.

In minutes he shifted her so she was lying on the sofa as he moved between her legs to unfasten her jeans and pull them off. Now the look in his eyes was filled with the same heat that was melting her. The temperature had soared and every inch of her body was sparking with ultra-sensitive awareness of his touch.

Watching her, holding her immobile with his heart-stopping gaze, he caressed her legs and gently spread her thighs, moving between her legs.

Aware how deeply she wanted him, Merry tried to summon caution, knowing in seconds they would both be beyond stopping. With stormy reluctance, she pushed against his chest. With all her being she desired this incredible, appealing man, yet wisdom urged caution. When she pushed lightly, he paused to look at her.

"I want you," he whispered hoarsely. His jeans bulged with evidence of his physical needs, but the hoarse note in his voice was filled with emotion.

Her heart thudded when she met his dark gaze. "I want you, Jason, but there are other things I want, too, and I can't have them. We have to stop now while we both can."

"I want you, Merry," he repeated.

Trying to get her breath, she pushed hair out of her eyes as she sat up. "This isn't what either one of us wants." She wriggled away from him, yanking up her T-shirt to hold it in front of her.

"I can't agree with that. It seems to me that it's exactly what both of us want." His voice was husky and raw. He stretched as if struggling to regain his control.

"My sister was devastated by a broken heart. I don't want the same thing to happen to me."

"Scared you might fall in love with me?" he asked with a challenging note in his voice.

She tilted her head to study him. "As scared as you are to fall in love—period. With me or anyone else."

His blue-green eyes turned icy, and she could feel a wall come up between them. When he wanted to, he shut himself off, keeping part of himself entirely private. Sometime in the past someone had hurt him badly, but he didn't want to share who or when or how with her, and she wasn't going to pry.

"Merry, I know this won't last and you know it won't. But why not enjoy the pleasure we find in each other? You've kissed guys before."

"Not like you," she answered honestly, and he drew a deep breath.

He moved to the end of the sofa away from her and raked his hair away from his face with both hands. Shaking his hair back from his face, he seemed to be gulping for breath.

She pulled her T-shirt swiftly over her head and jammed the wispy lace bra into a jeans pocket. As she stepped into her jeans, she saw him watching her intently.

"You're a beautiful woman," he said in a low voice.

"Thank you," she replied while her heart drummed with pleasure. She reminded herself he had told that to plenty of other women and not to be bowled over by sweet talk and hot kisses, but her heart wasn't listening to her head. When he caught her wrist lightly, she looked at him in surprise. The touch was casual, merely done to get her attention, yet it sent shock waves reverberating through her. Her body ached for his touch, for his kisses, for him to finish what he had started.

That wasn't something she wanted to let him know. Unable to summon words, she looked at him quizzically.

"Don't go. I'm not sleepy and I know you're not. Let's just sit and talk," he said, releasing her wrist.

"Just sit and talk—you promise?"

"Sure," he answered. He wiped his brow, beaded with sweat, and she still felt hot, too. "You say you want commitment, Merry. How much commitment?"

Surprised by his question, she sat and put her bare feet on the sofa, hugging her knees and facing him while she mulled his question.

"An affair—long-term? Marriage?" he asked. "What do you really want when you talk about commitment?"

"I'm very old-fashioned, Jason," she answered, knowing this would be the answer that would send him running or bring that cold wall higher between them. "I want it all. I want marriage. And for me, marriage is sacred and special."

"How'll you know when you meet the right person?"

"I'll know," she said quietly, trying to avoid looking too deeply into her feelings now as she studied the handsome cowboy facing her. She didn't want to admit the bald truth, but her heart was screaming her feelings.

"Just like that?" he asked quizzically. "Like lightning striking or what?" He sounded sincerely puzzled, as if she were the expert and he the novice in dealing with sex and love.

"I'll know the way anyone knows when she or he is in love. Surely you've been in love?"

He looked away, but not before she caught a strange flash that was almost a grimace. "I've loved, and I don't believe you if you tell me you've never been in love. You've dated, haven't you?"

"Yes. I haven't ever been truly, deeply in love. I don't want what you're accustomed to—flings that hold no strings of any sort. That's different."

He pulled at his jeans stretched across his knee and glanced at her, then looked back at his knee. His scowl hinted at some inner turmoil raging, but she remained silent, knowing if he wanted to say something to her, he would.

She put her head back against the sofa and closed her eyes, aware that they were at an impasse. And aware that she already cared too much about him. He was attracted to her, but did she want to give what was between them any chance to bloom? Could she risk her heart in dating him? Questions swirled in her mind and there were no easy answers except the one that tore at her every time she came back to it—go back to Dallas and get away from him. Even given the few people she knew in Royal, she had heard talk about Jason being such a playboy.

"Merry, I loved someone and I got hurt badly once," he admitted. She raised her head to listen. "I don't ever want to get hurt like that again," he said.

As she heard him talk about someone he obviously must have loved deeply, pain cut deep in her heart. At the same time, she realized he had just opened a part of himself to her that she suspected he kept closed from nearly everyone else.

"I'm sorry," she replied quietly. "Love carries risk and sometimes loving means hurting. Were you engaged?"

He was silent so long, she wondered whether her question had intruded too much. He shook his head finally. "No. When I was five, my mother left my father and my brothers and me. She remarried."

"Jason!" Merry said softly, shocked and caught by surprise, never guessing the shuttered looks had been because of his mother. A muscle worked in his jaw, and his fist was clenched on his knee. He had already told her his parents had been divorced, but she didn't realize those old hurts still plagued him.

"My father never got over her. Never. That's what hurt so damned badly. He loved her every day all his life, and he drank too much to drown his sorrows. It hurt to lose her, but that pain never diminished because my brothers and I had to watch our dad suffer. My brothers have had bad marriages, and I vowed I would avoid loving someone the way my father and brothers did. No commitment—no great hurt."

"Jason, love doesn't always bring hurt," she said, aghast at his dismal view of love.

"It makes you damn vulnerable," he said with rough cynicism.

"You want to go through life alone? There are so many joys when you share life. Children are wonderful."

"I have my nephews and I haven't exactly been lonely."

She hurt for him and she hurt for herself because she suspected his life was settled the way he wanted it, and he was in no danger of risking his heart. That realization spread pain deep inside her, because he was a strong-willed man who was old enough and experienced enough to know what he wanted and to control his impulses when he needed to. Hurt and sadness filled her. She was aware of the invisible barrier between them.

She thought about the living room that didn't seem to fit the rest of the house. "Your mother decorated the living room, didn't she?"

"Yes, and my dad never wanted to change it. It was the one room that held her touch. That and their bedroom, but he changed the bedroom. I suppose it was too painful for him the way it had been when she was here. But the living room is the same. I intend to change it, but I just haven't gotten around to it. None of us has ever used that room and now I don't give it much thought."

Merry moved close to him and put her arm around him. "I'm sorry. Do you remember her?"

He turned to look at her. He was only inches away now, and she realized moving close to hug him in sympathy was the wrong gesture if she wanted the attraction between them to cool. In the depths of his eyes, desire flashed as hot as a consuming blaze. When she met his gaze, her pulse jumped. His arm tightened, and he leaned the last few inches to kiss her.

Mouths touched, and that flash of heat and desire came, but along with it was more. Jason had just given her a part of himself that she knew he seldom had shared and it made the kiss more important. There was more of a closeness. And desire was building, igniting into heat that melted and shook her. The man could kiss. She didn't need to know his past to know she was with an expert. His mouth, his tongue were doing things to her, with her, that shattered her cautious resolve.

She wanted to kiss him in return, to give in return and to do to him even half of what he was doing to her.

She broke away finally, both of them gasping for breath. "We're going in circles. I should go."

He caught her wrist, turning her hand to kiss her palm. "Just stay and talk. We're not going to sleep. I promise I'll keep my distance if that's what you want."

"It's what I want," she said, knowing that wasn't the full truth at all. It was fast becoming less than a half-truth. She wanted him with so much of her being that it frightened her.

When she moved to the corner of the sofa, he looked amused. "I think I asked you if you remembered your mother. You don't need to answer me if you don't want to," she said.

"Oh, yes. I remember her," he replied. "Lots of memories that have grown fuzzy over the years and that I no longer try to dredge up. When I was little I thought she loved us all. I was wrong."

"I'm sorry you were hurt, because I think loving someone would be pretty wonderful."

"Yeah, if they always loved you in return."

"True enough. Are your brothers happily married now?"

"Yes. Ethan, who is thirty-five, has two boys from his first marriage and two from his second. Same with Luke."

"See, sometimes you can marry and live happily ever after."

"Maybe." A muscle worked in his jaw and she regretted his hurts and his attitude that she didn't think would ever change.

"So what's the next step with the disk?" she asked, trying to get away from a discussion of marriage.

"I'll give those copies of the files to Sheriff Escobar, to Rob—actually to several of the club members. I'll call them around seven to set up a meeting."

He scooted closer, stretched out his long arm and wound his fingers lightly in her hair. There were faint tugs against her scalp that should have been insignificant, but were not. Instead, desire that had been steadily burning, sparked and danced across her raw nerves. Her gaze drank in his thickly lashed eyes and sensual mouth. She longed to be back in his arms. Everything in her screamed that this man was important to her, yet she knew her reactions to him were dangerous to her well-being.

"If I meet with my friends tomorrow, will you stay here?"

"If you want me to. Yes."

"Is that a promise?"

"If it makes you happy, I promise to stay. I'd like to hear what everyone else thinks after you meet with them, but I should go home soon."

"You don't have to go yet. You rented an apartment, so you didn't plan on heading back to Dallas in the near future."

"Tell me again about the murder."

Jason talked softly, his hand stroking her nape or winding through her hair. The conversation shifted and changed and time passed until she glanced at her watch. "It's almost dawn."

"Well, we had a late start on the night."

"I'm going to bed." When she stood, he came to his feet.

"One good-night kiss, Merry," he said softly, a honeyed warmth that stole her resolve.

When he pulled her to him, she went willingly into his arms, relishing his lean, hard body against her softness. Mouths together again, and the same wild sensations and needs flaring. Winding her fingers in his hair and holding him, she kissed him passionately for a few minutes before stopping him.

"Now I go." She could feel his eyes on her as she left the room, and she suspected even though they had been awake almost the entire night, she would still have trouble sleeping.

She needed to move out of his house. Their kisses were escalating wildly into hot passion, and she didn't want that to happen. This was not the man with whom to become seriously involved.

"Sleep in, Merry," he called after her.

"Sure," she replied, glancing back over her shoulder at him. He stood with his hands on his hips, watching her as she walked away. His chest was bare, all hard muscles, tempting, special. The feel of him could turn her to quivering jelly. How easily she could turn around and walk right back into his arms and he would make love to her as long as she would let him.

Was she already falling in love with this tough, hard-hearted cowboy? Was he changing just a little? He had told her about his childhood pain, something she suspected he had told few people in his life.

"Don't get soft now," she warned herself, yet all she could think about was Jason: his touches, his kisses, his laughter, his sexy good looks. And beneath the scary moments tonight, the risks they had taken, she realized they had worked well together.

"That doesn't mean anything," she whispered, closing the door to her bedroom. "You've got me talking to myself, Jason Windover," she said. "Get out of my head. Get out of my heart," she added, moving to the bed to shed her jeans and shirt and slide beneath the sheet. She was exhausted, but not sleepy. Every nerve in her body was wired and she could still feel his hands on her, still remember too vividly his kisses. She'd better remember his dire views of marriage.

She came up out of sleep to bright sunshine pouring into the room. After she showered and dressed in cutoffs and a T-shirt, she went to the kitchen to find a note from Jason stating that he had gone to town.

Midmorning, he called, asking her to meet in him Royal for lunch and to help him select a new computer. Merry rummaged through her clothes, finally wearing jeans and a blue plaid shirt, letting her hair fall free.

They were to meet at the Royal Diner and when she turned to park at the curb, she saw Jason leaning against his pickup, waiting for her. As he straightened and sauntered over to open her car door, her pulse raced. How handsome he was in his black Stetson, jeans and a white T-shirt.

Over juicy hamburgers, she asked him about his morning meeting with other Texas Cattleman's Club members.

"I didn't get to talk to them. Dorian saw Sebastian and Will as they left the office and asked them where they were going and then wanted to go with them. I'll try again to talk to all of them when Dorian isn't present. But we were delayed getting together because the execs at Wescott Oil were busy with the law this morning. Will told me that someone broke into the place last night. Then, when we met at the club, Dorian was there, so little was said. Sebastian, Will and Dorian are eating lunch there now."

"What about Dorian?"

"He avoided my gaze most of the time, but a couple of times we made eye contact, and if looks could kill, I wouldn't be here."

"How can he suspect *you* of breaking in?"

"It may just be an old antagonism that has always existed between us. Anyway, I did get to talk to Rob and Keith as we left. I gave Rob and Keith copies of our disk. Keith was impressed with your getting into Dorian's files."

She shrugged. "That's my business."

"Well, after lunch you can help me get the right computer, and then please get it all set up for me, and in exchange…" His voice changed to a sexy huskiness that made her draw a quick breath and lose what little appetite she had. She waited while he paused and his eyes devoured her.

"In exchange?" she asked, prompting him and waiting breathlessly.

"Whatever your fee is plus dinner at Claire's plus a little romancing back at the ranch." He reached across the table to take her hand, stroking her knuckles with his thumb. "Want me to tell you what I'd like to do to you?" he asked wickedly in a husky voice.

"Not here. Not now."

"Later then," he drawled. "How's the evening sound? Do we have a deal?"

"I think so, yes," she said, knowing she was mush whenever he turned on his sexy charm.

"Good." He sipped his drink and looked at her partially eaten hamburger. "You're not eating."

"I'm not hungry."

"Neither am I. Not hungry for hamburgers," he said, his searing gaze telling her exactly what he wanted.

"Jason, we're in town in public."

"I don't care, and besides, we're just holding hands. It's not like I have you in my lap or any of a dozen things I wish I could do to you right now."

"Let's get that computer," she said, trying to get back to being impersonal, casual and merely friendly, yet finding it difficult to catch her breath.

He slid out of the booth, leaned down beside her. "If that's what you want, Merry," he said in a husky drawl that was like a stroke of his hand over her.

She waited while he paid for their lunches and then they left to shop.

She tried for the rest of the day and later, as they worked on the new computer, to keep distance between them and to keep things on an impersonal basis.

Around ten that night, Jason got a phone call; when he replaced the receiver, he looked at her grimly. "That was Rob. He's looked at the disk and he thinks the same thing we do—that more suspicion is pointed at Dorian. He said that Dorian knows someone was trying to look at his files. And Dorian suspects you, which makes him now suspect me. Rob said to be careful. Dorian probably feels safe at this point because there's nothing in his files incriminating enough to cause his arrest."

"Would he inherit Wescott Oil if something happened to Sebastian?"

"No. Rob has already checked into that, so I don't see what he has to gain. That's another big question—if Dorian is the murderer, what is his motive?"

Pondering the question, they sat in silence until they went back to the computer. At midnight, they closed it down and walked to the kitchen for a cool drink of lemonade.

Their good-night kisses escalated again until she stopped him and closed the door to her room at two in the morning.

She undressed swiftly, pulling on a frilly short red nightie and skimpy matching panties. In minutes she slid beneath the sheet.

Merry lay awake, knowing that she was falling in love with Jason. She just hoped she wouldn't leave Royal hurting the way Holly hurt, with a broken heart that threatened never to mend. And she knew she must move out tomorrow. She had already told Jason, and they had argued about it, but she had held firm and told him she was going to return to Dallas tomorrow.

Even though she desperately longed to stay, and she was curious to see what happened to Dorian, she knew it was time to go home unless she wanted a deluxe broken heart.

She was going to get out of the agreement to rent the apartment because now there was no reason to stay in Royal. She didn't want to harass Dorian further. It was time to stop seeing Jason, and she didn't want to risk her heart more than she already had.

She tossed and turned restlessly, knowing another reason to leave with the dawn—she couldn't say no to him much longer. More and more, she wanted to know him intimately, wanted his lovemaking. She didn't know what time she dozed into a light and fitful sleep.

An ear-shattering blast shook the house and her bed, tossing her to the floor.

Instantly awake and terrified, Merry jumped up and dashed across the room, yanking open the door. When she stepped into the hall, orange flames filled the east end of the house as an inferno roared and crackled.

"Jason!" she screamed.

Seven

The entire east part of Jason's house was in flames. She could feel the heat.

"Merry!"

Wearing only briefs, Jason grabbed her and pulled her to his room with him. He yanked on jeans and jammed his feet into his boots. Merry saw his T-shirt on the floor and grabbed it, realizing how she was dressed. Swiftly she tugged the T-shirt on over her nightie.

"C'mon, Merry!" he shouted, taking her hand again.

Bolting for the patio door, he paused at his desk to open a drawer and get a cellular phone and his pistol.

As he punched 911 and relayed a call for help, he thrust Merry to one side of the door. They both were flattened against the wall. The moment he broke the connection on his phone, he held her behind him with one arm and kicked open the door with his foot. He held his pistol at the ready.

When she realized he expected someone to shoot at them, her fright changed to an icy chill. Beyond the door was the dark night while behind them, she could hear the roar and crackle of flames and smell the acrid smoke. "Let me go first. You come right behind me," he said.

With the gun leveled, he ran through the doorway, and she followed.

The night was transformed. Men ran from the bunkhouse, dogs barked, and lights went on all over the grounds.

Jason sprinted ahead, and she followed him while he shouted directions to the first man to reach him. She glanced over her shoulder to see flames roaring and a huge column of black smoke billowing and mushrooming over the house.

At the sight of the conflagration, she felt weak and sick inside.

"Merry!" Jason snapped, catching her wrist and pulling her with him to run to his pickup. He opened the door and shoved her inside. "Stay in here and stay down so you're not a target."

"A target?" Startled, she looked at the men passing them on their way to the fire. How could she be a target now with so many people all around her? "There are men who work for you everywhere."

"A sniper could still get you."

Her shocked mind began to function. She realized then the possibility that the explosion had not been an accident and someone had been trying to kill her. Shivering, she looked at the brilliant flames. Anguish was stronger than fear as she remembered Jason's family heirlooms and antiques.

"Jason, your house!"

"It's just things, Merry," he said roughly. "We're alive. That's what's important, and let's keep it that way. Stay out of sight unless you want the press all over you."

"Jason, I thought it was a gas line."

"It was a bomb," he said bluntly.

"A bomb? Why?" The moment the words were out of

her mouth she thought of Dorian, of breaking into his computer. Was this because of last night?

She looked at the men who worked for Jason who were already fighting the fire. The first shocks receded further when she thought about the danger she might still be in, the police who would want statements and the press who were sure to arrive.

Jason was society and old money. The fire could be seen for miles and when word got out that it was from a bomb, the news would be nationwide. Her mother would want every tidbit and she would be livid to know that Merry hadn't called her the first moment.

Jason slammed the truck door, and Merry saw that he had pushed the lock.

She tried to stay low in the pickup so she would not be a target, yet she sat up enough to watch what was happening. All of the east wing and the center of the house were gone. If someone had been trying to kill her, he had bombed the wrong end of the house. If the bomb had gone off about three hours earlier, neither she nor Jason would have survived.

In spite of the stuffiness of the interior of the pickup and the balmy May night, she shivered. She heard the wail of sirens and she rolled down the window to get fresh air. The smell of smoke took her breath, and, with the window lowered, the roar of the fire was louder. Sparks shot high as wood crackled and popped.

"He's lost almost everything," she said softly. If it had been a bomb, it had been intended for her. She was the one to blame for Jason losing his family belongings and his house. She had stirred up Dorian who was a dangerous man, pushed him to this destruction and now Jason had lost so terribly much that could never be replaced.

She shook and wrapped her arms around her middle, unaware of tears streaming down her cheeks. Vehicles with flashing lights poured into the yard and men were everywhere. A news helicopter circled overhead while the media trucks rolled in.

Pumper trucks sent streams of water pouring onto the house. When pickups appeared and men jumped out, she realized Jason's friends and neighbors had come to help.

She could see Jason with the firefighters now. She wanted to go help, but she wasn't dressed for it and she wouldn't be that much more help now because there appeared to be at least fifty men fighting the blaze.

Firefighters, reporters, cameramen, lawmen, friends, neighbors and employees filled Jason's yard. The bright lights of the media lit up a place that now looked like a war zone.

Time was suspended. One moment she thought she had been watching for hours, the next, it seemed only minutes from the explosion until the flames had disappeared.

To her relief the fire was finally doused and the conflagration never reached the west wing of the house. Men still poured water over the smoldering ruins, but some of the volunteers began to get back into their pickups and go. When the television vans departed, she opened the door and swung her legs outside to get some air. She couldn't imagine being in danger now.

It seemed an eternity before she saw Jason's dark silhouette come striding toward her.

"You're making yourself a target."

"I'm safe," she replied. "What exploded?" she said, knowing his answer, yet praying his first assumptions were wrong, and it was a malfunctioning gas line.

"I told you earlier—and the fire chief agrees with me although they'll make an official investigation—someone detonated a bomb."

She shook her head in agony. "Jason, I'm sorry about your house. This is my fault for staying here. Whoever did this was after me."

"Forget it, Merry. I've made plenty of enemies before. And I wanted you here. I knew the risks we were running."

"I didn't." While she shivered, he put his arms around her.

"We can stay in the guest cottage. Let's go up to the house. I want to get a few things and then we can move. Some of the firefighters will hang around to make sure nothing flares up again."

As they walked toward the house, he draped his arm across her shoulders, and she walked close beside him.

"Merry, when the media interviewed me, I said I thought the explosion was from a gas leak."

"You told me—"

"I wanted that out in the news. I know Chief Blanton, and he only told them there would be an investigation into the causes of the blaze. It'll buy us some time before the truth comes out—if it ever does—that the blaze was caused by a bomb. I don't want that much attention focused on us yet. If Dorian was behind this, I don't want him brought into it in any way prematurely."

As they entered through Jason's bedroom, he removed his pistol and placed it on his desk. She could see down the hall and out into the night. Men moved around, and now, instead of walls and rooms, there was just open space. The smell of the fire and water was stifling, and she shook again.

"Jason, I did this to you. You could have been killed! Your wonderful house—"

"Merry," he said quietly, drawing her into his arms and tilting up her chin, "I keep telling you that we're safe. That's what's important. We're both all right. Things and houses can be replaced."

"You had all those family heirlooms and antiques. The family belongings can't be replaced."

"They don't matter that much. I told those guys that we'd be out on the porch at the guest house. Let's go down there. I want you to sit with me."

"Don't you want to look at the damage?"

"I've seen it with the fire chief. I've talked to my in-

surance agent and an adjustor will be out in the morning—
in a few hours, actually. I'll see the ruins more than I want
to.''

"How can you be so casual about it?" she asked,
amazed at his calm reaction.

"Because we're both alive. Let's get our things and
move. The guest house will smell better."

In a few minutes she had her purse and clothes. She had
pulled on shorts and kept on his T-shirt. When she joined
him, he had a bundle tucked under his arm. He put his arm
around her. As they walked to the door, he stopped to pick
up his pistol.

"You want to sit outside to keep watch, don't you?" she
asked. "You think he might come back."

"I don't think so, but I want to watch in case he does."

"We're talking about Dorian, aren't we?"

"I think so more than ever. You got into his computer
and he knew it," Jason replied as they crossed the yard to
the guest cottage.

"The minute the sun comes up, I'm going back to Dallas
and maybe your life can get on an even keel. You should
be safe."

Jason halted, turning her to face him. "I'm not worried
about being safe. I can get this place under guard and get
an alarm for the grounds around the house. You can't go
back to Dallas now. You could be in all kinds of danger."

"Stop it, Jason. You're scaring me. I have to go back
because if I stay here I put you at risk."

"Do you want to put your family at risk?"

"No!"

"Merry, I've been trained for this sort of thing. You stay
here." There was a steely command in his voice that made
her hold back any argument.

She nodded, and they continued walking in silence to the
guest house. Inside, when he switched on lights, she looked
at a spacious knotty pine room with Navajo rugs and Western art, bronze statues and forest-green leather furniture.

"You call this a cottage?"

"It's smaller than the house," he replied casually. "Come on, I'll show you where you can stay." She placed her things in a bright, cheerful bedroom with a brass bed and more Western art on the walls. Then she joined Jason on the porch. He switched off lights in the house and returned, bringing two chilled bottles of pop.

They sat close to the house with their backs only inches from the wall. A shaggy black-and-tan dog wandered up, sniffed Merry's feet and moved to put his head on Jason's knee.

"This is Tiger."

"He doesn't act like one."

"If you see him in daylight, you'll see he has stripes." The dog curled at Jason's feet and placed his head on Jason's boot.

"I guess he does like you."

"You didn't give a rip whether I had dogs that liked me or not when you asked that first night. You were planning your escape, weren't you?"

"As a matter of fact, I was. I wanted to know what I might run into outside your house."

"Now that I've had time to think about it—if Dorian did cause the blast tonight, you may not have been the target. Any computer disks we had could have been what he hoped to destroy."

"I hope you're right."

"Think about it. I met with my friends, but nothing was said about anyone stealing anything from Dorian's computer. He didn't even mention that anyone got into his computer. I didn't mention disks. I asked Rob to take a disk to Sheriff Escobar. If Dorian followed me, he would know I didn't go to the police. Besides, the files by themselves are not that convincing—it's just that with the suspicious things Dorian has done, the computer files are more evidence that points to Dorian."

"If all he intended to destroy were the computer files—why do it when we were home?"

"He might have wanted to send a message. He might have wanted to scare you off. Scare both of us off, maybe. If he knew which end of the house we were in, then all he wanted was to destroy my disks and my computer—which he did. But Rob and Keith already have copies."

"It makes sense, Jason. Unless he knows nothing of the layout of your house."

"I suspect whoever set the bomb knew the layout as well as we knew the layout of Wescott Oil. As a matter of fact, I had a party several months back and the Texas Cattleman's Club members were out here. Dorian would know his way around here reasonably well."

"Maybe I'm not in as much danger then."

"Maybe, but let's not take chances. Not for a while."

As they talked quietly, she noticed Jason kept his pistol on a table beside him and all the time they talked, he was gazing into the dark night.

"Mr. Windover?" A fireman spoke from the dark shadows to the east of the porch, and Jason stood.

"I'm here." He left her, crossing the porch and striding to the fireman to talk quietly to him.

"Jason," she heard another man say and join the two of them. From the jeans and boots he wore, she judged the other man worked on the ranch. She could hear their low voices, catch phrases as they talked. Tiger had followed Jason and sat at his feet. Another dog meandered up to sit beside them.

Finally Jason shook hands with the fireman and thanked him again. As the man left, Jason turned to his employee and they talked in even lower voices. When they parted, Jason came back to join her.

"Let's go inside."

"What about keeping watch?"

"My men are spread out all around here. No one will get past them tonight. I promise—you're safe here."

He draped his arm across her shoulders, but then he paused and turned. "Ben," he called.

A deep voice came out of the darkness, and she could see the cowboy yards away.

"Call the dogs and keep them with you."

As a whistle broke the stillness, both dogs trotted away and Jason led her inside.

He closed and locked the door and then switched on a small lamp. As he crossed the room to her, the look in his eyes made her forget the events of the night. Her breath caught and each step closer he came, her pulse jumped another notch.

"Jason," she whispered while her heart thudded.

"There's something I want to know, Merry," he said solemnly. His voice was husky, causing more jumps in her pulse.

A thick fringe of black lashes framed sexy blue-green eyes that blazed with desire. He placed his hands on either side of her face while he gazed down at her. "Tonight, when we talked right after the fire, you sounded like you care what happens to me."

Her heart thudded at the implications of his question. She could answer it flippantly—tell him that she would care about anyone being hurt. That was the answer if she wanted to walk away. But not one tiny inch of her wanted to walk away from him. The night had changed her, brought everything around her into sharper focus. Made her more aware of the frailty of life and of the gifts of love. She could give him one of those casual answers now, or she could tell him the truth.

"Yes, I care a lot."

Something flickered in the depths of his eyes and as he inhaled swiftly, his chest expanded. "Ahh, Merry," he said softly.

He leaned down to kiss her, and her heart thudded. She had been terrified for his safety tonight, crushed over the damage he had suffered—loss and danger that she had brought on him. In spite of all his losses, his concern had been their safety and the safety of the men who worked for him.

This tall cowboy was incredibly special to her, and she was thankful he was safe. She was thankful that they were both alive. Wrapping her arms around him, she leaned into him as he embraced her.

When his lips touched hers, she kissed him passionately in return. Her kisses were hungry, a confirmation of life, a sharp awareness of how precious life was—and how special Jason was to her.

All her reservations fell away. Someone had tried to kill them tonight, yet they had survived. They were alive and caution and reason seemed foolish where her heart and Jason were concerned. Priorities shifted. Life was infinitely precious, and love was a gift to give.

Jason was special, and she wanted to show him, wanted all of him, wanted him as she had never wanted anyone else. They had been on the brink of death tonight, and now she wanted an affirmation of life, a chance to love.

Considerations and terrors of the night vanished.

Her tongue went deep, stroking his as he kissed her passionately, and she slid her hands over him, feeling his body, all hard, lean planes and corded muscles. Excitement exploded in every nerve in her body.

As he trailed kisses along her throat, his hands peeled away her T-shirt. Her nightie went with it. When she unfastened his jeans, he cupped her breasts, looking down at her. His hands were large, dark against her pale skin, his fingers warm, setting her aflame.

"You're beautiful," he whispered hoarsely, and her heart thudded.

All the time he balanced on one foot and tugged off a boot, then yanked off the other one, tossing them aside, his gaze never left her. Clothing fell swiftly, but invisible barriers seemed to be tumbling as well.

He made her feel like the most desirable woman on earth.

When he straightened, she pulled away his briefs to free him, drinking in the sight of his strong male body that left no question of his desire and readiness.

His large hands cupped her breasts again, and his thumbs circled her taut peaks. Pleasure swirled while she clung to him, feeling the thick muscles of his upper arms. His strength was exciting, his touch electrifying.

She closed her eyes, letting him caress her, wanting his hands all over her, wanting to touch and know him.

She slid her hand to his chest, trailing her fingers down over his flat, muscled stomach, touching his manhood.

"Merry," he ground out her name when her hand closed around his thick shaft.

He swung her into his arms to carry her to his bed. She was dimly aware of light spilling from a hallway, of a four-poster bed, a rocker, but surroundings were dreamlike and unreal. What was real was warm flesh against warm flesh, kisses that sent her temperature soaring, looks that made her tremble.

Why did she feel she belonged in his arms forever? She ran her fingers along his jaw, feeling the bristles, aware of all he had been through in the night and all he had lost, aware too of that walled-off part of his heart that was keeping him from truly loving and being loved. Didn't he realize that real love could heal hurts?

Placing his knee on the bed, Jason lowered her gently and leaned down to kiss her breast, his tongue stroking her nipple as he sucked and teased. Exquisite sensations stormed her senses, and she gave herself to him. His hands were everywhere, his tongue driving her wild.

"Merry, I've wanted you so damned badly," he whispered. His magic words were as seductive as his caresses. He turned her on her stomach, trailing kisses from her nape to her ankles. He stroked between her thighs and she rolled over, coming up to kiss him hungrily, knowing no matter how much he desired her, she wanted him more.

"Let me love you, Jason," she whispered, certain that he would never realize the true depth of her request.

She did want him with all her being, even though she was honest enough to know that he would never love her deeply in return. Tonight she wanted to give and take and have it all. Tonight, she was willing to risk a broken heart.

Strong shoulders, smooth back, narrow waist, his manhood: she wanted to explore and touch and kiss all of him. As she did, she heard his groan and was surprised that he shook. She was amazed what she could do to him, expecting him to be jaded and accustomed to women as expert at loving as he. But that wasn't the case. He was coming apart in her arms until he grasped her and shifted her roughly. "Merry—"

He cradled her in his arms, kissing her as passionately as she kissed him. His hand caressed her thigh, sliding to her inner thigh and she opened her legs to him. While she caressed him, his fingers trailed higher, reaching the juncture of her thighs and then touching her intimately. He stroked her, taking her to a new height, finally lowering her to the bed. He moved down to trail his tongue where his hand had been. He was between her legs, watching her as he kissed her.

She closed her eyes, arching and gasping, lost in scalding sensations, yet fully aware this was Jason who was loving her and who wanted her.

Thought spun away while lights flashed behind her closed eyes, and she dug her fingers into his shoulders, arching and wanting more of him, wanting him deep inside her.

"Jason!"

She rocked with spasms that only made her want more. With an effort, she moved, turning to take his manhood in her hand, to kiss and caress him until he groaned and shoved her back to the bed, moving between her legs.

"Are you protected, Merry?"

"Yes, I'm on the Pill."

He was on his knees between her legs and she inhaled, feeling breathless as she looked at him. Virile, handsome, so incredibly sexy, he knelt, poised, ready to love her. His blue-green eyes were dark with need, a look on his face that heated her blood to boiling. Then she closed her eyes as he lowered himself, the velvet tip of his shaft teasing, moving against her.

With a cry, she wrapped her legs around him and arched beneath him, pulling him closer. His mouth covered hers, and she clung to him, writhing and wild with her need.

Jason tried to hold back, to drive her to the highest point of need. Sweat covered his body, and his pulse drowned out all sounds. She was silk and softness and a marvel to him. She was a wildcat, more passionate than he could have imagined.

The fire in her auburn hair only hinted at the fire in her body. He kissed her deeply, wanted to plunge himself into her softness, to feel her moving beneath him, crying out in ecstasy.

He slid into her and then felt the barrier where he hadn't expected one. *She was a virgin.* Something he hadn't considered. He couldn't take her or hurt her. He raised his head to gaze down at her.

Her eyes opened, dark, yet caught with pinpoints of fiery, age-old desire. "Jason…" she urged.

"Merry, I don't want—"

"Love me," she said, moving against him, arching her hips, her hands sliding over his bottom and pulling him closer while her legs tightened around him. "Jason, now. I want you."

"I don't want to hurt you. I don't—"

"I *do* want," she whispered. "Come here, now," she coaxed.

He couldn't argue. He had given her a chance and his control was flying away. He thrust slowly into her, feeling the barrier, knowing he had to be hurting her.

She gasped and he kissed her, stopping whatever sound

was caught in her throat. Then the barrier was gone, and he went deep inside her, moving slowly, trying to keep from hurting her. Thought and effort shattered, and he had to move, to take her completely.

Merry clung to him, feeling torn apart, swamped for an instant in pain, but as he moved, the pain was replaced by a driving need and she moved with him. She held him tightly, crying his name, yet the cry was only a sound in her throat because his mouth covered hers. While they rocked together, desire thundered in her.

"Merry!" Jason cried, his arms around her, and then his head lowered again, and he kissed her again while all she knew were wild sensations tearing her apart before she crashed into release.

Rapture exploded in her, carrying her further into oblivion while Jason shuddered with his release.

She held him, moving with him, their hearts pounding in unison. He kissed her as hungrily as before and she returned his kiss as passionately, feeling a bond between them now, an intimacy that she could not have known before.

"Merry, my love," he whispered, smoothing her hair away from her face.

Even while his words thrilled her, she knew better than to believe them. The man was in the grip of passion and she would not hold him accountable for what he said to her now.

She trailed her fingers down his back, wet with a sheen of sweat. Her hand moved up then to tangle in his thick, coarse hair.

He raised up to look at her, a slight frown on his brow. "Did I hurt you?" he asked solemnly.

She traced the outline of his lips, trailing her finger to his jaw and feeling the slight stubble of his beard. "Only a little."

"Next time will be better. I promise."

"Next time?" she asked, arching a brow.

"Yeah, next time," he said, turning on his side and taking her with him. He let out a long sigh and held her close against him. "Merry. Did you get that nickname because you were always cheerful?"

"No. When she was a very small child, Holly couldn't say Meredith and my name became Merry." While she talked, Jason's fingers trailed over her. He stood and leaned down to scoop her into his arms.

"Come here, darlin'. We'll shower."

He carried her into the bathroom and set her down in the shower, stepping in with her to close the door. He tilted her chin up to look at her quizzically. "You told me you were on the Pill, but you were a virgin."

"It was because of medical reasons. The Pill regulated me."

He nodded, satisfied by her answer as he turned on the water and it sprayed over them. In minutes, as they rubbed each other's bodies, desire rekindled until he turned off the water and stepped out, taking a towel to rub her dry. "I want this to last and be good for you, to really take time."

"Jason, you take more time than we did before and the sun will be high over the house!" she said, wondering how near dawn it was now. And then, as he moved the thick terrycloth towel lazily across her nipples, down between her legs, over her bottom, she forgot about the time altogether.

She caught the towel to dry his body, relishing touching him, exploring every fascinating inch of him. He carried her back to bed to kiss her from her mouth to her ankles while his hands drove her wild. And then she returned the loving, kissing him all over. He moved between her legs and took her slowly. This time sensations rocked her, causing her to arch against him as she clung to him, her hands splayed on his smooth back.

Intimacy united them. She was one with him, body and soul, a deep joining that forged bonds. Their shared, hot kisses held promises of love.

They moved wildly together and finally crashed over a brink. Merry settled slowly with Jason sprawled over her. She wanted to feel the weight of his body and wanted to be one with him as long as possible.

When Jason rolled over, he pulled her into his embrace, his legs tangling with hers, her head on his chest. He held her tightly against him with one hand while he stroked her back with the other.

"You're a very special woman, Merry."

His words strummed across her heart, and she raised her head slightly to kiss his chest, looking into his eyes.

"And you are a very special cowboy," she answered, wanting to say so much more.

He brushed her damp forehead and lifted locks of hair away from her face. "We'll go shower in a little while, but right now I just want to stay here and hold you close."

"I want you to hold me," she whispered, holding him in turn, wanting to take away his past hurts and toss aside his fears of love, yet knowing she could only take him as he was.

She put her head down on his chest and held him tightly, shutting out reality and problems as long as she could. "Whatever the future holds, neither one of us will forget this night for the rest of our lives."

"No, we won't." Jason kissed the top of her head while he continued to caress her with his free hand. He was still stunned by the night, by Merry. He had never been with a virgin, had never wanted to be, but now it was as if he were seeing the world in a whole new way. He felt overwhelmed. Now he understood why some put a price on virginity; it was as if Merry had become his woman. His completely. He told himself he was being ridiculous, but his heart wasn't buying that. She was *his* woman, and she had given him the very special gift of herself.

When they were in the throes of passion, he knew he had called her "love"—something he had never done before. And he knew he wanted her to an extent he had never desired any other woman.

He remembered their conversation last night—an eon away—yet her words were too clear: *How'll you know when you meet the right person?*

I'll know.

Just like that? Like lightning striking or what?

I'll know the way anyone knows when she or he is in love. Surely you've been in love?

No, he hadn't ever been deeply in love, never experienced what he was beginning to feel now for Merry. Was he falling in love? How had she gotten past his defenses so swiftly and so thoroughly? This five feet of feisty female had stormed into his life and knocked him off his feet in every sense of the word.

He shifted onto his side to look at her. He couldn't get enough of touching or kissing her. *He wanted her again. Now.* Suddenly, when he had expected to be satisfied, to have gotten her out of his system, he wanted her more than ever. More than he had just hours ago.

"I could devour you," he said in a husky voice, kissing her throat. "Come here, Merry," he said, standing and picking her up to carry her to his shower again. This time they soaped each other slowly, until both were breathless, gasping with need. They rinsed off, their hands sliding over each other's slippery bodies. Jason braced himself against the wall of the shower, spread his feet and lifted Merry up to let her slide down slowly onto his hard shaft.

She held him, moving and crying out with pleasure, finally feeling a burst of release. Afterwards, she put her head on his shoulder. "You won't have to carry me to the shower this time. We're already here."

"My legs feel like pudding. We're getting to that bed before you have to carry me back to it."

She smiled at him as he set her on her feet, and they washed. As soon as they toweled each other dry, he carried her to bed to pull her close into his embrace again.

"Jason, will we know when the sun comes up? Your shutters are closed."

He groaned. "I don't want the sun to come up. I have an appointment with the insurance guy. Some firemen will be back to gather more evidence and check things over. I don't want to leave this room or let you go. I want to stay right here with you in my arms, in my bed for the next week."

"Sorry, cowboy, that's impossible."

He rolled her over and propped his head on his hand to study her. "Maybe I can try keeping you here, and we can just ignore everyone."

"No!" She sat up and reached for the shutters that were all tightly closed.

He caught her arm and kissed her wrist, looking at her solemnly. "Maybe I'm falling in love, Merry."

Merry's heart thudded at the words, but she reminded herself she was with Royal's number-one playboy. She had heard about his reputation. She smiled and patted him.

"That's nice, Jason," she said.

He drew his finger down her cheek. "I mean it. Don't patronize me."

"I wouldn't think of it," she said, kissing him lightly. His arm tightened around her and his lips touched hers, brushing so lightly. Then his mouth opened hers, kissing her deeply. Tongues touched and stroked while her heart pounded.

She pushed against him. "Wait a minute." She glanced at the clock on his desk. "Jason, that says it's almost eight in the morning. That's late for you to be getting up."

"Don't care. Come here, darlin'," he said in a husky voice.

By a quarter before nine, Jason groaned and stood. "I have an appointment in fifteen minutes." He caught her chin. "Merry, you're safe here, so you stay here today. I don't see how he would dare try anything again as long as you're out here and there will be someone around all the time. Promise me you'll stay.''

''I will,'' she said, knowing it was probably useless to argue, and Jason didn't seem the least concerned about risk to himself.

He picked up his cellular phone and switched it on, punching in a number. ''Rob, this is Jason. Yeah, we're okay. I need to see you and the others when we can. Definitely without Dorian.''

Eight

As Jason drove away from his ranch, he wanted to turn around and go back to be with Merry. The need he felt to be with her surprised him because the intensity of it was a unique experience. At the same time, his feelings tied him in knots.

He didn't want to fall in love. Not the forever till-death-do-us-part kind of love. Yet being with her was the best thing that had ever happened to him. He couldn't wait to get back to the ranch and see her, hold her and kiss her.

Even the danger and the boldness of Dorian—if Dorian was the one—couldn't take his thoughts off Merry.

Since childhood he had sworn he would never love deeply, never be caught in the trap his father had been in, loving a woman and becoming vulnerable. But now nothing seemed the same. If loving Merry made him vulnerable to hurt, he couldn't help it. He was as out of control as a shooting star. If this was love, he was in, head over heels, and it seemed damned good and right.

She was a beautiful, sexy woman. She was intelligent, fun to be with, kindhearted and exciting. He wanted to be with her all the time, and the thought of her walking out of his life made his breath catch.

He was the only man in her life. The first, the only. That thought tugged at him, and made the bond between them even stronger.

Stunned by his reactions, he marveled at how his feelings for her had changed his whole perspective on life.

In town, the day seemed interminable. Jason couldn't set up a meeting with the others from the Texas Cattleman's Club until tomorrow morning, but they knew about the bomb. Everyone in Royal knew his house had burned, but only his close Cattleman's Club friends knew the truth. The only information the media had still indicated a possible gas leak, and that suited him.

Through the busy day Jason struggled to concentrate on the problems facing him, yet Merry was constantly on his mind. It amazed him to feel this way—as if Merry were the most important person on earth. Earlier that day, he had almost walked in front of a moving car. His attorney had been with him and had reached out to stop him. Hal Worthington had chalked Jason's fog up to the night's calamity, talking nonstop to Jason about his loss and how sorry he was about the explosion and fire.

Jason had barely listened as Hal had rambled, and as soon as they parted, Jason called the florist and ordered a dozen red roses, saying he would pick them up on his way back to the ranch.

On his way to an appointment, he paused in the lobby of a building, finding a corner where he could call Merry undisturbed.

Her voice was lilting, making him remember the night too clearly.

"Merry. I wanted to talk to you."

"I'm glad you called."

"I've made reservations to take you to Claire's tonight."

"You don't think it's dangerous for us to be in Royal?"

"No, I don't. If the bomber was Dorian, I suspect he was after the disk or giving us a warning. I'll keep you safe, I promise."

"You can't promise me absolute protection."

"I'll do my best. Darlin', this morning seems a year away instead of hours."

"Yes, it does," she answered in a softer tone of voice.

"I hate being away from you, and I'll be home as soon as I can—probably half-past five before I can get there. I've gotta run now, but I had to talk to you."

"Thanks for calling," she said in that same low, breathless voice that made him want to cancel all the rest of his afternoon appointments and go home right now.

"'Bye, Merry," he said, wanting to say so much more, continually shocked by his intense reaction to her. As soon as she returned his farewell, he broke the connection, pocketed his cellular phone and left for a meeting with his accountant.

In a daze Merry replaced the receiver and walked to the bedroom they had shared the night before, staring at the bed while her thoughts spun vivid memories. She was in love with Jason, but she wasn't falling for any wild promises or lines from him because this was old stuff to him. He was a playboy and oh-so-clearly had let her know he didn't want to be involved in a serious commitment.

In spite of knowing about his past and his reputation, she loved him, and a broken heart seemed inevitable. She knew that she needed to move out of his house and get some distance between them because she was going to have to resist his sweet-talking, sexy charm if she didn't want to become as devastated as her sister.

In the meantime, she would be here tonight and she was going out with him this evening and for the next twenty-four hours, she was going to close her mind to the future.

At half past five she heard his pickup and saw him stop at the main house and get out to talk to one of the hands, then he climbed into the pickup and drove to the guest house. She wanted to run and throw herself into his arms. She looked down at her cutoffs and red T-shirt. Her hair was clipped behind her head and she smoothed wayward tendrils back into place.

The door of the pickup slammed shut, and as she watched his ground-eating stride, her pulse jumped. In his black Stetson, jeans and a white shirt, he looked sexy and appealing. In his hand was a crystal vase with a dozen deep-red roses.

He opened the door and tossed away his hat as his hot gaze met hers.

"Hi," he said in a husky voice. "I brought you flowers."

"They're beautiful," she said without taking her gaze from his. He set them on a table as he crossed the room to her.

Her racing pulse accelerated, and then she was flying to fling herself at him. The moment they were in each other's arms, Jason walked her backwards toward the bedroom.

While they kissed, her hands were all over him as much as his were all over her. She hadn't known it was possible to desire someone the way she did Jason. Still kissing him, she unbuttoned his shirt and tugged it out of his jeans frantically, barely aware when he pulled her T-shirt over her head and tossed it away. In their slow walk to the bedroom, clothing was strewn willy-nilly.

"I want you, Merry," he whispered hoarsely. "I haven't been able to think about anything else all day."

She wound her fingers in his hair, kissing him while her other hand trailed over his chest.

He cupped her bare breasts to fondle and kiss her while she closed her eyes and moaned with pleasure. Urgency tore at both of them. Her hungry need for him overwhelmed her. She caressed him as he lifted her onto the bed and moved between her legs, lowering himself and entering her swiftly.

She arched beneath him, clinging to him and moving with him, giving herself completely to him. She ran her hands over his smooth, muscled back, down to his thighs, memorizing each inch of him. Body against body, united, hearts beating together. How she wanted it to be forever!

When they crashed with release, ecstasy filled her and in that one moment, she held him, knowing they were one.

"I couldn't wait to see you," he said when their breathing slowed to normal. He held her close in his arms, his fingers smoothing her hair from her face. "I'm torn between wanting to take you to Claire's tonight and wanting to stay right here in bed and love you all night long."

She drew her fingers through his hair, feeling the thick strands, letting her hand slide down to his strong shoulder. "I suspect you'll get hungry later."

"Hungry for you," he said, nuzzling her neck. "Reservations are for half-past-eight. That gives us some time." He turned to kiss her throat. She ran her hand over his muscled back, still covered with a sheen of perspiration. She couldn't get enough of him either. She wanted him in her arms, loving her, more than she wanted anything else. And she really didn't care whether they went to Claire's or not.

"Merry, the club has an annual charity ball coming up—will you go with me?"

She looked into his thickly lashed eyes and kissed him lightly. "Yes, I'll be happy to go with you. What's the charity?"

"Sebastian headed up the ball this time. He decided to make a bet with all of us. This was back in his bachelor days. All of us were bachelors then."

"Sorry to interrupt your story, but who is *us?*"

"Sebastian, Rob Cole, Keith Owens, Will Bradford and I are the group. The bet was that the last bachelor left standing—since most of those guys are marriage-minded—"

"But one isn't," she interrupted him.

Smiling, Jason kissed her lightly. "Maybe. Maybe I'm changing."

"Like tigers lose their stripes. Go on. Tell me about this last bachelor."

"The last bachelor left standing will enjoy a 'consolation' party during the ball and get to choose the charity for the gala."

"So what's your favorite charity, Jason, since you'll win this bet, hands down."

"You're really sure about me," he said, studying her and toying with locks of her hair.

"You've made your feelings clear. What's your charity?" she insisted.

"There's a program for kids who need help with literacy. That's the charity I'd name."

"That's a good one."

"Actually, three of the guys are married now. Will, Sebastian and Rob. So it's down to a contest between Keith and me."

"Well, I know who'll win, and a lot of little kids will be helped."

"You're so sure about me," Jason repeated. He rolled over to prop his head on his hand and look down at her. "This would be nice to always come home to," he said solemnly, and Merry's heart lurched. Instantly she told herself to not be taken in by lines he may have said too many times.

He kissed her hungrily, a kiss that heated her from her head to her toes and made her forget the annual ball or the last bachelor or anything else they had talked about. She was lost in another dizzying spiral of lovemaking.

Two hours later Merry finished dressing and walked out to find Jason standing waiting in the living room. The moment she stepped into the room, her breath rushed out. In a dark suit and white shirt, Jason looked even more handsome and commanding than ever.

His gaze lighted with pleasure as he looked her over, making her tingle from head to toe.

"Darlin', we may go to Claire's more often," he drawled. "You're gorgeous, Merry."

"Thank you. I could say the same about you."

She wore a simple black dress with a V-neck and a low-cut back. It was a sheath, clinging to her figure and hitting her just above the knees.

He crossed the room to tilt her face up. "Now I've lost all appetite for anything at Claire's. What I'd rather have is you, but I'm going to take you out at least once."

"I think that's the best idea."

"No. My best idea is bed."

She linked her arm through his. "Let's go, Jason." She touched the bulge beneath his coat and patted his side, looking up at him questioningly while problems rushed back into her life.

"I might want my pistol," he said to her unasked question.

"That makes me want to stay home."

"You'll be safe," he said with a determination that gave her a chill.

"I'm glad I know you now and not when you were living a different life."

"Whether in the CIA or out of it, I'm still me. And I usually don't carry a weapon here in Royal, but the situation changed when someone blew the end of my house away."

They walked in silence to the car and he held the door. "Jason," Merry said after they were driving from the ranch, "if Dorian has a good alibi for the night of the murder, that leaves him out as a suspect. Other things, like the electronic journal and his shady past, indicate it was him, yet if he was sitting in the Royal Diner the whole time, he's not the killer."

"Laura Edwards testified that he was at the diner. The

police checked her background, and she seems honest enough.''

''That alibi really lets Dorian out.''

''Probably, but it doesn't hurt to keep looking. You never know what you might uncover or where.''

It was half past eight when they walked into the elegant entryway of Claire's. The lighting was dim and the carpet thick. A couple leaving the restaurant headed toward them and paused.

''Hi, Jason,'' the tall, handsome man greeted Jason. Merry looked at an attractive black-haired woman standing beside the man.

''Merry, this is Pamela and Aaron Black, some friends of mine. Meet Meredith Silver she's from Dallas.''

''I think we've met,'' Aaron said with a twinkle in his green eyes.

Meredith blushed as she nodded. ''Aaron was outside the Texas Cattleman's Club when I first arrived and was searching for Dorian Brady,'' she explained to Jason.

''How's the baby?'' Jason asked.

''As wonderful as ever,'' Pamela answered, smiling. ''She's almost seven months old now.''

''I just happen to have her latest picture,'' Aaron said, grinning and whisking a picture from his wallet. ''This is our Amy,'' he said, and Merry looked at a picture of an adorable baby girl with huge blue eyes and wisps of black hair.

''She's beautiful,'' Merry remarked.

''Thanks. We think so, too,'' Aaron replied proudly.

''Put the picture away,'' Pamela said, laughing. ''Aaron is immersed in fatherhood and he pins everyone down to show them pictures and tell them about Amy.''

''That's great,'' Merry replied.

''Yeah, it is,'' Jason added. ''Thanks again, Aaron, for coming to help fight the fire the other night.''

''Glad to do it. You'd do the same for me. If you need any more help with anything, let me know,'' he added solemnly, and suddenly Merry didn't think he was talking about fires or ranching at all.

"I will."

"I hope you find the cause."

"We're working on it," Jason replied grimly, and Merry was certain Aaron knew more about the fire than the general public did. "When things settle and I get the house rebuilt, you two will have to come over and bring Amy for a cookout."

"Thanks," Aaron said. "We'd like that."

"It was nice to meet you," Pamela told Merry.

"We'll let y'all get to dinner," Aaron said, taking his wife's arm and heading toward the door.

"He's a fellow rancher and a fellow Texas Cattleman's Club member. He used to be in the diplomatic service. The worldly diplomat married the local school marm. I doubt if Pamela has ever been one hundred miles out of Royal. At least, not until she married Aaron."

"They seem very happy."

"Yeah, they are happy. This past year Aaron has been the happiest I've ever seen him."

"So marriage isn't always all bad," she teased.

"I never said it was bad. I just said it wasn't for me. And that was all before I met you."

"You come up with statements like that as easy as breathing," she accused, determined not to be taken in by a charming expert at seduction.

"I mean what I say, Merry," he said solemnly, and she tried to ignore the thud of her heart. "Here's the maître d'," Jason said, turning to the man.

In minutes Jason and Merry sat at a white-linen-covered table with a candle and a single rosebud in a crystal vase. Jason ordered steaks for both of them, but when hers came, Merry could barely eat. All she wanted was to be back in Jason's arms.

Halfway through dinner she sipped her red wine and lowered her glass, slanting her head. "What? You're looking at me and not saying anything, but something's on your mind.''

"Yeah, it is," he said in a husky voice. "I was thinking about you, us, home together. That's where I want to be."

She drew a deep breath and last shred of her appetite fled. "Someday I'll have to tell you no, but it isn't going to be tonight."

"I don't ever want to hear no from you," he said solemnly.

"We won't argue that one now," she said. "This night is special."

He picked up her hand and brushed a kiss across her knuckles. "It's damn special. Ready to go home or do you want to finish your steak?"

"I'm ready, Jason," she said in a sultry voice, and his eyes darkened as they did in moments of passion.

He motioned to the waiter and in minutes they were in Jason's car, headed down Main and out of town. She saw Jason adjust the rearview mirror and watch it often.

"What are you looking at?"

"Traffic. We've picked up a tail. Why don't you get down."

Chilled to think they might be in danger, she slid low in the seat, loosening her seat belt.

"Don't take that seat belt off. We may be in for a bumpy ride. You hang on, because I'm going to do a turn in just a minute."

"Are you certain we're being followed?"

"Yep. I am."

Suddenly he jammed the brakes, spun the car in a U-turn on Main Street and sped back the way they had come. Merry half slid off the seat and scrambled to get back up.

"Dammit," Jason snapped.

"What's wrong?" she asked, sitting up to see what was happening.

"He's gone. Whoever it was moved quickly. When I turned, he shot across the street into an alley." Jason whipped down Main, spun around a corner and raced down the next street.

"You may hear sirens in a minute. You're more than over the speed limit," she said. "That wild turn you made in traffic on Main should have brought the law."

"He's gone," Jason said and hit the steering wheel with his palm. "Damn. I wanted to see who it was."

"We're safe and now we're not being followed," she said, resting her hand on Jason's thigh. The moment she touched him, she tingled with awareness that drove all thoughts of danger away. Jason looked around at her and drew a deep breath.

"We're going home," he said roughly.

They drove out of town on back roads, and, as town lights faded and darkness enveloped them, Jason drove swiftly. He held Merry's hand on his thigh. He wanted to stop, pull her into his arms and make love to her here, now, in the car. But he knew they would be safer to wait until they reached the ranch where alarms and guards would be a protection.

He listened while she talked, but his thoughts were only half on what she was telling him. He was thinking about being followed, and then his thoughts shifted to their discussion of the Cattleman's Club ball and the remarks on marriage. He'd told her that he wasn't the marrying kind. But was that really the truth?

Was he in love with Merry Silver? He knew he needed to sort through his own feelings, but he had never before been this way about a woman. Never wanted one with a need that was insatiable, a craving that was impossible to fully satisfy.

He thought about meeting and talking to the Blacks. Aaron looked happier than he had ever before in his life and Jason had known Aaron Black since childhood. Hell, all his married friends looked happier. And Pamela Black looked radiant. Jason had known Pamela merely as an acquaintance, but he had always thought her rather plain. She didn't look plain now. *Radiant* was the best description of her. And Merry tonight in her black dress had stolen his breath away. She was gorgeous, alluring, sexy. He thought about his past doubts and fears of commitment; they seemed to be melting like fog in summer sunshine.

Would Merry ever walk out on her family?

The question seemed absurd. No matter how tough the situation, he didn't think she would walk out on a commitment or responsibility. Look at her taking off work to take a little revenge on the man who'd hurt her sister so badly.

He had spent a lifetime swearing he would never marry. How could he throw over years of solid conviction after just a few days of knowing someone? Merry had turned his life upside down, stolen his heart, stormed his senses. He liked everything about her, which was crazy because he hadn't liked a lot of things about her when he met her. She was fiery, impetuous, impulsive, feisty. Not his type of woman.

Keep telling yourself that, he thought. But that wasn't what his heart and mind and soul were shouting inside him. He wanted her, needed her, *loved her*. There it was. He was in love with a woman—deeply, truly in love for the first time, in spite of his playboy reputation and the many previous women in his life. None of those affairs had been serious. Not one.

He looked at Merry, who sat serenely gazing out the window at the dark Texas countryside that was nothing but flat land and mesquite trees. How could she have become so damned necessary to him? So special. *He was in love.* He wanted to reach across the car seat, pull her beside him and kiss her.

Acknowledging what he felt was amazing. Never had he expected love to happen to him. He had guarded against commitment, fought it, shrugged it away as something that happened to other people, but would not be a part of his life. Now love had become vital.

He wanted to tell her exactly how he felt, but right now, speeding home through the empty night, was not the place for a very special announcement.

She would want children. He had never given children a thought because he had never expected to fall in love, much less marry. A baby with Meredith. Their baby. The notion was awe-inspiring.

But before that was love. Glorious, fire-and-dynamite loving. He remembered her in the throes of passion, her legs around him as she cried out his name. He increased the speed of the car slightly because he wanted to get her home.

He couldn't keep from glancing at her repeatedly. She seemed oblivious to his glances, and he wondered what was running through her mind.

"What are you thinking?" he asked finally, his voice a notch deeper because his thoughts were erotic.

"About Dorian having an alibi, yet so much points to him. And I'm thinking about being followed tonight. Whoever bombed your house, if the person was sending a warning—why follow us? If it was Dorian after the computer disk—why follow us? Unless whoever it is really intended to harm us and failed with the bomb," she added.

"We're safe. Don't worry about it, and no one is following us now."

"No, but if they know who you are and who I am, then they know exactly where we're going right now."

"I'm watching and I'm armed."

"Somehow that doesn't reassure me. I don't want to get into a shootout."

"We won't. Whoever this is, he or she doesn't work that way. So far, with the exception of Eric Chambers, there's been no direct confrontation."

"I'd call bombing your house about as direct a confrontation as you can get."

"Let me worry about the danger. I was hoping you had

other things on your mind.'' He stroked her nape lightly while he watched the road.

''What things?''

''Us. Making love,'' he answered in a husky voice.

She leaned close to him to flick her tongue out and kiss his ear. ''We did that, mister, not much over a couple of hours ago.''

''Merry,'' he groaned, ''this is the longest ride home I've ever had.''

She laughed softly and ran her fingers up his thigh. ''You keep your attention on the road.''

In the early hours of the morning Merry snuggled against Jason, who held her close. He lay on his side, his head propped on his hand as he studied her. She had a sheet pulled high under her arms, but her shoulders were bare, her hair a riot of silky auburn locks cascading over her pale skin. Jason ran his finger lightly along her hip, covered by the sheet.

He was in love, and he thought again about their conversation.

How'll you know he's the right person if you haven't gone with him some first?''

I'll know.

Just like that? Like lightning striking or what?

I'll know the way anyone knows when she or he is in love.

He had told her he had been in love, but it wasn't like this. This love was the real thing. He understood her now when she said she had never been truly, deeply in love. It shocked him to find himself head over heels in love. He had guarded against it, but had he really been preventing falling in love, or had it simply been that Merry had not yet come into his life?

Now the urge was growing stronger by the hour to get some kind of commitment from her. He didn't want her to go back to Dallas.

And even though she hadn't declared her love, she must feel it because she had given herself completely to him and only to him. He kissed her shoulder, then nuzzled her neck, wanting her fiercely again, as if they hadn't made love through most of the night. He pushed the sheet down to fondle her breast, lowering his head to take her nipple in his mouth and kiss her. When she stirred and moaned, he raised his head to look at her. Her eyes slowly opened and she smiled at him, wrapping one arm around his neck.

"I love you, Merry."

"You're nice, Jason."

He caught her chin in his hand. "I'm really in love with you."

She smiled at him, a mysterious, feminine smile that left him unable to discern what she truly felt. "I'm glad."

"I don't think you believe me."

"Of course I do, to a degree," she said, twisting to turn onto her back to wrap both arms around his neck and pull him down to her. "I'll show you, Jason."

It was noon the next day before he kissed her goodbye.

"I have appointments all afternoon, and at four, I'm meeting with Sebastian, Rob, Will and Keith to tell them what we found in Dorian's computer files and about my fire."

"Be careful in town."

"I will, and you stay on the ranch and don't disappear." He kissed her hard and long and then released her. "I have to break some bad news to my friends about our suspicions. See you tonight."

She watched him stride away and thought about his declarations of love and reminded herself not to be taken in by them. Once again, she told herself that she needed to pack and go home, back to her regular life instead of this life that had turned into a dream.

Nine

Late in the day, Jason sat in the meeting room at the Texas Cattleman's Club. The air-conditioned room was cool and quiet. Iced tea and cold beer had been served. Will and Sebastian had come from work and had shed their suit coats and ties and rolled up shirtsleeves. Leaning back in one of the comfortable leather chairs, Keith was in chinos and a green knit shirt while Rob was in jeans and a blue Western shirt like Jason.

Jason looked around the circle of solemn faces.

"Thanks for coming. I want to bring all of you up to date. I asked you to keep this meeting confidential," Jason said. "We've cut Dorian out of the meeting."

"Is there a good reason?" Sebastian asked with concern in his gray eyes, and Jason suspected Sebastian still wanted to believe the best about his half brother even though it was growing more difficult all the time.

"I think there is," Jason answered. "Merry and I got into Wescott Oil—"

"You're the burglars?" Will asked incredulously.

"Where and how is Merry?" Rob asked.

"She's fine and she's out at my ranch," Jason replied evenly.

"Well, she's not escaping now," Will observed with amusement. "Is there some reason for this?"

"Hey, maybe *I'm* going to be the last bachelor left standing," Keith said, staring at Jason. "I might win that bet after all," he said.

"You can't beat our resident playboy," Rob remarked, watching Jason closely even though he was grinning. Rob tilted his head. "That's right, isn't it?"

Thoughts flitted through Jason's mind as he hesitated before answering, a mistake, because instantly all of them were teasing and asking questions.

"Our playboy bites the dust," Rob said. "The wildcat gets her man."

"The wildcat lassos the cowboy, hog-ties and drags him to the altar," Keith said.

"She won't have to drag me," Jason replied, and whoops of laughter and disbelief burst from his friends. He grinned and waited for them to settle.

"You're going to be the last bachelor," Rob said to Keith.

"Well, not quite so fast," Jason cautioned. "The lady hasn't said yes. I haven't asked her yet."

"Oh! Sorry, Keith," Sebastian said, "The truth comes out. I can't see our playboy popping the question."

This brought more teasing which Jason put up with patiently.

"Okay, y'all," he said finally. "Enough's enough. We didn't meet to discuss my love life—"

"Which would fill two or three volumes," Rob interjected.

Jason waved his hand. "I'll keep you posted. In the meantime, Keith, you're not exactly the last bachelor, although I hope to change that soon."

"Will wonders never cease?" Will said.

"You better get to planning that ball and thinking about your charity, Keith. Looks like we've got our man," Sebastian said.

"For just a minute let's discuss why I called y'all here and why I asked you to keep this meeting quiet," Jason said.

"I think we were talking about the burglary at Wescott, which I now find out was done by you and your lady love," Will said.

"Yes," Jason admitted.

"I knew about their plan," Sebastian admitted. "I didn't tell you, Will, because I thought that the fewer people in on the plan, the better. And this way, when you got the news, your reactions were normal and sincere."

"Merry got into Dorian's computer files—"

"Dammit, I thought we had those so secure no one could get into them," Will snapped. "We had to open Eric Chambers's files for the police."

"Well, she got into them in about five minutes," Jason informed him dryly, and Keith laughed.

"That's embarrassing because we sold Wescott some of its software and set up the programs. The wildcat's not so crazy after all," Keith added.

"Anyway, we were interrupted because Dorian came to the office. Merry copied some files and got enough to indicate that Dorian kept an electronic journal. There's a reference that made it sound as though he was blackmailing Eric Chambers."

"Let me interrupt," Keith said. "Rob and I have copies. I can give you one, Sebastian, and then you can pass it to Will. All right?"

"Sure."

"The next thing…" Jason continued. "A statement went out on the news that the fire at my place may have been caused by a gas leak. There was no gas leak. I gave that to the press. The fire chief said that they were investigating what caused the fire, which was the truth on his part. He just didn't elaborate. But we knew that night that the explosion was caused by a bomb.''

''Why you?'' Sebastian asked. Before Jason could answer, Sebastian answered his own question, ''Was it because Meredith Silver is at your place?''

''We don't know, but one possibility is that it was done to wipe out my computer and any disks that were copied at Wescott Oil the other night.''

''That would have to be Dorian,'' Keith said.

''He's got that damned alibi for the murder,'' Rob reminded them. ''Laura Edwards swears he was sitting in the Royal Diner the whole time that Eric Chambers was murdered.''

''Yes, but Laura Edwards seems very much in love with Dorian,'' Will remarked dryly. ''There's always the possibility that he has pulled the wool over her eyes, and she's covering for him.''

''A lot points to Dorian,'' Jason reminded them grimly. ''And we have a mole in our group, so, more than likely it's one of us.''

''Damn,'' said Sebastian. ''If it's Dorian, I brought him into our group.''

''If it's Dorian,'' Jason said, ''then he's caused you a world of grief when you were trying to be a brother to him. We're all going to be sorry about that.''

A grim silence fell over the group. ''So where do we go from here?'' Will asked.

''I think we need to set a trap of some kind for Dorian,'' Rob suggested. ''If Dorian's the murderer, he's done too much and gone too far. Whoever is behind all this has killed Eric Chambers, tried to frame Sebastian, bombed Jason's house—''

''If it's Dorian, there's a possibility he has taken money from Meredith Silver's sister. She doesn't have proof though.''

''Dammit again,'' Sebastian said. ''I brought him into

our group, moved him into my business, my circle of friends. I did everything for him. Why would he do this? What's his motive? If something happens to me, he won't inherit what I have. He'll be worse off with me gone than if I'm alive. I can't see what motive he has, and he has a sound alibi.''

Another silence followed and Jason tried to keep his thoughts from drifting to Merry.

"Okay, back to where we go from here," Will said. "I agree with Rob that we need to set a trap. Let's think about what we can do, because we have to be careful. He's aware we suspect someone in our group, so that narrows suspicion to him instantly. He may get desperate, and if he's the guilty party, he's already murdered once, so he has nothing to lose if he does it again."

"Sorry, but I have to go. I have an appointment," Will announced, standing.

"Everybody think about what we can do to set a trap," Jason suggested. "We'll meet again—a week from now, same time, all right?"

All heads nodded and Jason stood.

"And Keith," Will said, grinning, "you consider what charity you want. I think our playboy is losing his title."

"I might be," Jason admitted, thinking about Merry and how long it would take him to get to the ranch.

"I hope you're not so in love that you can't watch your back," Rob cautioned, moving beside him as they left the club.

"I'll be careful. I have guys guarding the ranch. Even though he may have just been after the computer and disks, I'm having an alarm system installed for the grounds around the house."

"Maybe, but you don't know. She's annoyed him no end. And we need to find out for sure if it's Dorian. If we're chasing the wrong person, we're wasting time and putting everyone in more jeopardy."

Rob paused to face Jason. "We talked about setting a

trap for Dorian. There is something that we might do that wouldn't involve a lot of risk. It might be just one more bit of proof. You could get Merry to confront him here in Royal.''

"Oh, no! I'm not jeopardizing her—"

"Look, this wouldn't be as dangerous as what the two of you did breaking into Wescott Oil. That could have got you shot.''

"Not in Royal. I don't want her in danger." Wind caught locks of Jason's hair as gazed at his friend.

"She's in danger just living at your ranch. Do you want to catch this guy or not? She isn't afraid to go after him.''

"All right," Jason relented reluctantly. He knew Merry wasn't afraid, and she would want to do whatever she could to help trap Dorian. ''What's your idea?''

"With Sebastian's help, because he works with Dorian and knows where he is from eight to five, we could arrange a seemingly casual meeting during the day between Merry and Dorian. They could encounter each other with people around and in daylight. I've got a mini-recorder that she can drop into her pocket and pick up every word he says. I don't need to tell you about those devices.''

"I hate to have her anywhere near the creep. It'll just be one more goad to a man who may be desperate now.''

"We need some proof. If he would own up to knowing her and her sister, that would be one more arrow pointing to guilt on his part. It wouldn't tie him to the murder, but it would show that he's been lying to us.''

Jason mulled the plan over. He wanted to refuse, yet he knew Merry would agree to doing it without hesitating one second.

Rob continued, "If they met in broad daylight on the streets here in town, I don't think he would do anything. I could be in a car not far away. I wouldn't let her out of my sight and I wouldn't suggest it if I thought it would put her in any danger.''

"You don't need to bother watching her because I will.''

"If you want both of us to watch, even better."

Jason nodded. "I don't want to take any risks, and if she doesn't want to do it, that's it."

"Good," Rob said while satisfaction lit his eyes. "I know what her answer will be. You weren't there when she stormed into the club. The lady is determined, and she didn't act as if she would be scared of Old Ned himself."

"She might not be," Jason agreed with a sigh, "but that doesn't mean I want her at risk."

"I swear I'll watch her and keep her safe."

"Both of us will. I'll ask her about it tonight."

"I'll call Sebastian. Tell Merry thanks."

"You're so damned sure of yourself."

"Nope. I'm sure of her. I think she's a good match for you, my friend. She'll keep you hopping."

"She already does. I think Dorian's the one, but then, I never have liked the guy. If it's him, he knifed Sebastian in the back after all Sebastian did for him."

"Yeah, but if he won't inherit, then why did he kill?"

Jason shrugged and headed for his pickup. "That's what we have to figure out. See you."

"Hey, Jason, wait up," Keith called and jogged across the lot to catch up with Jason.

"Does Meredith need work?" he asked.

"She's a freelance programmer."

"She must be damned good at what she does. I could use someone like her in my business. I'd like to talk to her about a job."

"Get in line and give her a call. You know my number."

"Get in line?"

"Rob wants her to do something for him. Go ahead, call her."

"I will. Thanks."

"I'll tell her that you'll call."

"Great. See you later." Keith turned to go to his car and Jason slid into his pickup, forgetting about Keith instantly as his thoughts turned to Merry.

He didn't want her to confront Dorian ever, but he would leave the decision to her because Rob's plan didn't sound like it would put Merry in jeopardy.

As Jason drove along Main, he thought about her. He wanted to get her a ring. He wanted to buy her everything, wanted to give her the world. He was in love, and it was scary and marvelous and amazing. When could they marry?

This was May, and if he could have his way, they'd get married next week, but Merry had a big family and he did, too, so he suspected a wedding would be a major event. Could he get her to stay at his ranch until then? He wanted her with him constantly. He was more amazed at himself than his friends were. He had never, ever expected to be in love, never known he could feel like this about a woman. He was dazzled, unable to concentrate on anything else very long before she filled his thoughts. He loved her and he wanted to marry her—the sooner the better.

Jason drove to a jewelry store, and an hour an a half later he drove out of town with a ring in his pocket, roses beside him and a bubbling eagerness to see her again.

As he raced home, Jason glanced out the window and realized he had passed the road to his house. He groaned, swung in a U-turn and headed home.

"Woman, you better marry me before I lose it completely," he grumbled, knowing now it would be ten minutes longer before he would see her.

Merry lolled in a tub of sudsy water while she contemplated her future. She had to make decisions, because, since arriving in Royal, Texas, her life had changed completely. She needed to move out of Jason's house, get back to work and go on with her life.

Three more days. She would give Jason three more days and then she had to pack and go. She didn't think she would be in any danger if she moved back to Dallas. She lived in a gated apartment that was as secure as the one that she had rented here in Royal seemed to be. Right now, for tonight, she didn't want to think about leaving Jason, and she put it out of mind. The time would come soon enough.

She finished bathing, dried her hair and dressed carefully in a blue sundress with a halter top and full skirt. She slipped into sandals and looped and pinned her hair on top of her head.

Wayward tendrils escaped to curl around her face and she left them, making a face at them in her reflection in the mirror.

It seemed like forever before she heard Jason's pickup, and this time she did go out to meet him, flying into his arms. He caught her up, kissing her hard and long as he carried her into the house and kicked the door shut. He set down the vase of roses and turned to Merry.

"It's been an eternity," he said in a breathless voice and pulled her into his embrace.

An hour later Jason held Merry close against him. "I'll cook steaks unless you'd prefer I'd take you to town to Claire's again."

"Actually, the steaks right here sound like a deal."

"Steaks it is. Let's shower first."

She moaned softly and hugged him. "If we shower together, there won't be any steaks for hours."

"How hungry are you?"

She gave him a sultry, heated look that made him groan. He stood and scooped her into his arms and carried her to the bathroom and it was another hour before they were seated in the kitchen over thick, sizzling steaks and baked potatoes covered with melted butter and sprinkled with chives.

Glasses of red wine sat on the table along with warm slices of bread, crisp asparagus and slices of juicy red tomatoes.

"How was your meeting today?"

"I almost forgot. Keith Owens is going to call you. He wants to offer you a job with his company. He was impressed that you got into Dorian's computer files, because Keith's company sold software to Wescott and helped them set up some of their programs.''

"He's offering me a job here in Royal?''

"Yes. Think about it, all right?''

When she smiled at him, Jason thought about the ring upstairs in a drawer beside the bed. Their dinners were only half eaten, but he had lost his appetite.

"Come here,'' he said, taking her hand. "Let's dance.''

He already had music playing, and he pulled her into his arms.

In his arms Merry moved with him as if they had danced together forever. They danced into the family room with its hardwood floor. In her sundress, her back and shoulders were bare and he caressed her while they danced.

When she raised her head, he leaned down to kiss her, wanting her as fiercely as he had when he had driven to the ranch earlier today.

"Merry, I love you,'' he whispered.

Something flickered in the depths of her smokey eyes, but she merely gazed at him solemnly and then stood on tiptoe, pulling his head to hers.

They kissed and Jason wanted to bury himself in her softness. He unfastened the buttons on the sundress and let it fall away while she tugged his shirt out of his pants.

She took his breath with her luminous gray eyes, hot kisses and fiery hair. He wanted her with a desperate urgency, but he wanted to make love to her for hours, to make it as good as possible for her, to drive her wild.

He peeled away the bits of lace underwear she wore and shed his own clothing, tossing it aside to pull her down on the sofa and kiss her from head to toe.

Merry was lost in sensations, aware of Jason murmuring endearments as he kissed her, trying to turn them off in her mind, to give herself to passion and feeling and not let her heart be talked into believing a dream he was weaving around her.

Hours later, they loved in the big bed until they lay exhausted, wrapped in each other's arms while their racing hearts slowed.

He kissed her tenderly, moving beside her and stroking her face. "I love you, Merry. Really love you. For the first time in my life, I'm truly in love."

She put her fingers over his lips. "Jason, it's good. Let's leave it that way."

"You don't believe me, but I'm telling you the truth."

She smiled at him, determined not to be completely taken in by the words. The man was the ultimate playboy, the consummate lover, and she wasn't falling for a line of love promises made in the throes of passion or right after loving.

He turned, opening the drawer beside the bed to fumble in the drawer. He rolled back over to place a small black box on her bare stomach.

She stared at it with curiosity, realized it was probably a jewelry box. Pulling the sheet beneath her arms, she sat up. Jason took the box from her hand and gazed at her solemnly while he opened it.

"Merry, I love you. Will you marry me?" he asked, leaning forward to kiss her lightly.

Stunned, Merry looked at the beautiful diamond catching glints of the soft light in its sparkling depths, and then she looked into Jason's blue-green eyes that made her heart thud. Everything inside her cried out acceptance. *If only...*

Ten

Unable to answer him, she looked down at the diamond. Why did it have to be this way? Inside, she hurt, a pain that spread and deepened, and she wondered whether it would completely consume her. She kept staring at the diamond until Jason tilted up her chin, and she gazed into his solemn eyes.

"I love you, Merry. You've changed my life and how I feel about things. How I feel about love."

She kissed him, long and slowly, barely aware of the salty taste of her tears, knowing that she was going to be heartbroken, but also knowing there was only one answer to give him.

"Tears?" he said, leaning back and framing her face to wipe away her tears with his thumbs. "Merry, I love you. I think you love me," he said, watching her intently.

"Jason, we haven't known each other long enough. This is too fast. Last month I didn't know you. Days ago you told me in no uncertain terms that you would never marry."

"Well, I hadn't fallen in love then. My life has changed because of knowing you."

"It's too soon to really know what you feel deep in your heart."

"I think you're the one who said something about you'd just know when you fell in love. Well, that's the way it's been with me. I know what I want and how I feel." He gazed into her eyes in a long, probing look. "Tell me you don't love me."

"You know I can't tell you that, but this is too fast. I don't want to rush into an engagement, rush into a marriage. Last month you were certain you'd never marry. You've spent a lifetime—your adult lifetime—going from woman to woman. For you to really know your feelings is going to take time."

"No, it isn't," he answered, and her pulse jumped because she wanted with all her heart to believe what he was saying.

"If we love each other, time will prove it."

"I don't want you to go back to Dallas. I want you here, just as you are now. I want you in my arms, in my bed every night. I want to come home to you, to call you when I need you, to have someone to share everything with."

"Jason, I want that so badly that I don't dare think about it."

"Let go and trust me. Acknowledge what you know you feel."

"You can't be so sure so fast. I don't know if you've done this with every other woman you've—"

"I haven't asked another woman to marry me," he interrupted her gruffly. "I swear to you, Merry, I've never told a woman I loved her. Not once, not ever. Not even as a teen. There was always a part of me that stood back and held back and kept quiet."

"Oh, Jason," she said, knowing that withdrawal was from old hurts, but that didn't mean he was so completely certain now. "I don't think you can change quickly and really know how you'll feel a year from now or two years from now. This is way too fast, way too superficial.''

"There's nothing superficial about it. I know to the depths of my soul, Merry. I've never been this way before. I know for certain.''

"Then date me and show me. There hasn't been anything normal or routine about the time we've been together—the bomb, I'm away from home, I'm living here—''

"The intimacy and the upheaval ought to allow us to know each other better and know our feelings better. In a crisis all civilized veneer is stripped away and what's real is left. And that's what we've seen of each other.''

"Maybe, but I think we need some time and space. I can't believe you really know your own heart. No one can have a complete turnaround the way you have. Not this fast. Jason, when I marry, I want it to be forever.''

"I do, too. And I know my heart. I know what I feel for you. I love you.''

She closed the ring box and placed it in his hand. "Maybe in time, Jason. Not now. There's no way you can convince me that you deeply, truly love me. You were far too convincing only a short time ago when you said you would never fall in love, never marry.''

"I didn't really know you then.''

"You don't really, really know me now.''

"I think I do. And what I don't know, I want to find out.'' He held her face with his hands. "Dammit, woman, I love you. I want you to marry me.''

She gazed into his eyes, blazing with determination and desire. He pulled her closer to lean forward and kiss her long and hard.

"Marry me,'' he urged after a lot of kisses.

She moved away, wrapping his fingers around the ring box. "We can talk about it, and you can see how you feel after we get to know each other better.''

He caught her chin with his hand and his eyes burned

into hers. ''I know exactly what I want. I love you, darlin'. And I'll convince you of it.''

Her heart thudded, and she couldn't resist pulling him to her, taking them both down on the bed and kissing him wildly. Letting go with kisses and lovemaking, she couldn't get enough of him or give enough of herself to him. There were no barriers here, no holding back. Time did not exist. Love was all-encompassing, and she could pour out her love for him.

The next morning, Jason left the house shortly after dawn to round up steers to take to market.

A lot of the ranch work Jason did was from his pickup, but today he and the men were going on horseback. At the corral he saddled his gray horse and swung into the saddle, riding out to join the others.

All through the day, unless his attention was completely on his work, he thought about Merry and how to convince her he knew his own feelings. In late afternoon before he returned to the house, he flagged down his foreman.

Almost seven feet tall and thick through the shoulders and chest, Dusty Grant strode over to him.

''I want you to handle this sale tomorrow.''

''Sure,'' the blond giant replied, taking off his hat and wiping sweat from his forehead and neck with a red bandana.

''I'd like to take a few days off. I'll be around the house if you need me, but I want some time off.''

''Sure, boss. It's fine. Day after tomorrow you were going to that horse sale.''

''I can do that, but you take over the rest.''

''Will do,'' he said. ''Men are standing watch around the clock.''

''Until we find out who planted that bomb, keep a watch going. I don't want anything else to happen. Thanks, Dusty. I asked Henry to fly us to Houston tonight, and we'll be back sometime tomorrow.''

''Sure thing.''

Jason turned and headed for the house. He was flying Merry to Houston to dinner tonight and they'd return home tomorrow. His pulse speeded in anticipation. She knew they were going out to dinner, but he wanted the flight to be a surprise, so he hadn't told her.

He stretched out his stride, hurrying to the guest house, wanting to be with her, something he had yearned for since he'd told her goodbye this morning.

He crossed the porch and reached for the door as she stepped outside and into his arms. He caught her up and embraced her tightly, kissing her as he walked them both inside and kicked the door closed. Reaching behind him, he turned the lock. He wanted her desperately. ''I'm dusty and hot—''

''I don't care,'' she whispered, and his pulse soared. She was cool, smelling sweet and enticing, so soft in his arms. He couldn't wait, peeling away her clothes and shedding his. His hands shook with haste and need. She was soft, wild, magical. In minutes he lifted her off the floor and she locked her legs around him while he entered her. Urgency drove them, and he felt as if it were the first time all over again.

''Merry! I love you. My love, my woman,'' he whispered, wondering how long it would take to convince her of the depth of his feelings.

Thoughts vanished as he relished loving her, swept into ecstasy with her and wanting it never to end.

Later, after they had showered, he carried her to bed to hold her close in his arms until they had to dress to leave for dinner.

He waited in the small living room, finally hearing her heels clicking, and then she walked through the door. Sexy and beautiful, she paused, her gaze warm enough to melt him as he drank in the sight of her in a clinging red dress with her hair looped and pinned on top of her head. Stray tendrils hung down, framing her face. As always, he was tempted to forget dinner and just go back to bed. But he wanted to court her and win her over, and taking her out was part of that.

"You're beautiful," he said, his voice husky. He couldn't keep his reactions to her from showing. Nor did he really want to.

"You look very handsome, too," she said breathlessly. "Sure you want to leave?"

"Hell no, I don't want to do anything except make love to you, but I want you to have some special moments besides when we're in bed. So let's go."

She took his arm and it wasn't until they turned and drove up to the small jet waiting at the Royal airport that she raised her eyebrows. "So what's this?"

"We're going to Houston for dinner and dancing."

She smiled and leaned close to kiss him. "Sounds great. Another very special evening with you."

"Let's see how special we can make it," he said quietly, wishing she would come home wearing his engagement ring.

Jason tried to be his charming best through a lobster dinner with glasses of chablis and a flaming dessert. The restaurant had an indoor waterfall and a pond with blooming lilies. There was a deserted dance floor because the combo would not commence playing for another hour. In the meantime, soft piano music added to the cozy atmosphere. Their table had candlelight, white linen and a vase of pink tulips and daisies.

His appetite had diminished since he'd met her, and it wasn't any stronger tonight.

"Jason, this is exciting and wonderful, but life goes on. Monday, I have an appointment with Keith. Whatever I do, I need to move out of your house."

"Merry—"

"Wait and let me finish," she said firmly. "I will either go back home to Dallas or I'll accept Keith's offer and move into the apartment I rented here in Royal."

"I don't want you to go."

"I have to. I can't keep staying at your house."

"I wish you'd marry me, and that would settle it. I love you. Can't you see that?"

"I'm flattered, but I don't think you know what you feel."

He groaned and wanted to pull her into his arms and stop all this nonsense by making love to her until she acknowledged what they both felt.

His past had caught up with him, something he had never given a thought to before. He sipped his wine and wondered how much time it would take to convince her that he meant what he was saying. This was a problem he had never expected to have. She was sexy and sweet and unfortunately, as strong-willed as he was. He took her hand, feeling her smooth, soft skin and looking into her smoke-colored eyes that held flames in their depths.

Until Merry, he had never found a female he couldn't charm or seduce or win over to his way if he wanted to. She was moving out Monday. The announcement was like the plunge of a knife into his heart. She might go back to Dallas. He hurt and he didn't want her to go. He didn't want time or distance between them, but he knew it was pointless to argue with her about it.

"You're a challenge, Merry. And you've been one since that first night at the club."

She smiled at him, a twinkle in her eyes. "You need a challenge every once in a while."

"What I need is you," he answered, his voice becoming a rasp. The band began to play and he glanced at the dance floor, standing. "Come dance with me," he said, taking her hand and wanting her in his arms.

As she danced with him, he tightened his arm around her waist, holding her close, frustrated because he couldn't convince her of his feelings.

He wasn't going to let her go, but he damned sure didn't want to court her for a year or longer and that's what she seemed to be hellbent on him doing. He kissed her soft cheek, blew lightly in her ear, and wished she could see that he knew his own heart.

"Merry, I've told you this before, but I'll say it again. I know what I want."

"If you're really in love, then time will prove it, Jason," she answered so sweetly he wanted to gnash his teeth and swear.

The music changed to a fast number and he watched her move around him, a flame in her red dress. He wanted to pull her hair down and peel her out of the dress and it took a major effort of will to keep dancing instead of taking her back to the hotel suite he had reserved for them. He didn't want to think about Monday and her leaving.

In the early hours of Monday morning, Merry lay awake in Jason's arms. Neither had slept well, loving most of the night, yet both aware of the deadline she had arbitrarily set. She knew the most difficult thing she had ever done would be to move out in a few hours. She had turned down his ring and proposal, now she was moving away from him, but she knew she had to.

This morning at half-past ten, she had an appointment with Keith Owens. It would have to be a very good offer to pull her away from her freelancing. She turned on her side to look at Jason as he slept. Locks of his unruly black hair fell over his forehead and his cheek. His muscled chest was bare, the sheet down below his waist. Her heart thudded, and she wanted so badly just to move into his arms and say yes, she would marry him, and forget all caution. But she didn't want major regrets later.

His arm was draped over her. He held her always in the night, moving her close against him, even in his sleep. She brushed locks off his forehead. "I love you," she whispered.

Sleep was impossible, and she was still awake when Jason stirred, tightened his arms around her and pulled her closer to kiss her.

They loved long and leisurely, yet with an underlying urgency. When she finally dressed to leave the ranch for her appointment with Keith, time was running out and she had to rush.

With her things packed and in her own car, she hurried through the house to find Jason waiting in the kitchen. He stood when she entered the room.

His gaze raked over her simple blue suit. "You look gorgeous."

"Thanks, Jason. I hope I look professional. I have to run or I'll be late to meet Keith."

"Keith will understand if you call and change the time."

"I'm keeping my appointment. Kiss me goodbye," she said, walking up to him with her heart thudding.

His arms wrapped around her tightly and he pulled her close, kissing her long and taking her breath. She knew she should stop him. He was drawing out his kiss, rekindling desire that smoldered all the time. She pushed against him. "I have to go now."

"No, you don't really," he said gruffly, his blue-green gaze intense and tearing into her. "And you could come home to me afterwards."

"We've been over that." She headed toward the door and he moved with her, holding the door of her car and closing it behind her.

Jason leaned down to take her chin in his hand. "I'll meet you for lunch at the Royal Diner after your interview."

When she nodded, he stepped away from the car.

She started the motor, shifted and drove away. Glancing in the rearview mirror, she saw Jason standing with his fists on his hips, his feet spread apart while he watched her drive away.

She hurt and wondered if she had just tossed aside a wonderful future. Was she making an incredible mistake by not saying yes and following her heart and rushing into marriage?

Tears streamed down her cheeks and she wiped at them hastily, not wanting to go to a job interview with clothes wet from tears. She didn't particularly care about the interview, but Keith Owens had sounded as if he could make her an interesting offer, and he was very complimentary about her skills, even though he was basing his opinion on her getting into Dorian's files.

When she walked into his office, he stood to offer her his hand. She looked into friendly brown eyes. "I'm glad to meet you again under better circumstances."

He laughed. "You stirred us all up, but we need that sometimes. Have a seat." Dressed in dark slacks and a button-down short-sleeved broadcloth shirt, he was casual in appearance and approach. He moved away from his desk, turning a chair to face her and looking relaxed. "Thanks for getting your résumé to me so quickly."

"My sister sent a copy to me, and it was easy to send one on to you."

"Your résumé is impressive. But getting into Dorian's files is even more impressive. We have an opening I think you would be perfect for."

She listened while he talked, and all through the interview, she kept thinking that if she took the job with Keith Owens's firm, she would live in Royal and not be separated from Jason.

The longer they talked, the more interested she became.

"Would you like a tour of the place?" he asked, and she nodded, standing when he did.

As they walked through offices, in between introductions and explanations of various departments, he gave her a brief history of his firm. When they finally returned to his office, he faced her.

"Any more questions?"

"I've asked you everything that's come to mind."

He grinned. "You don't know what salary I'm offering."

"Some of the other considerations are more important, and I knew we'd get to salary before I left."

He named an amount, and she whistled. "That's a very good salary."

"That's to start. In six months we'll review things and then you may get a raise. I hope you'll think about working here."

"I'm interested, and it's a very attractive offer," she replied. She stood, offering her hand. "Thanks so much. I'll be in touch with you soon with my answer."

"Good, Meredith."

"Call me Merry. I go by Merry more than Meredith."

Keith walked to the office door with her and told her goodbye again. As she crossed the shaded parking lot, she mulled over her choices. Stay here and date Jason and see what happened or go back to Dallas and date him on weekends or whenever they could get together. The job sounded worthwhile and the salary was fabulous.

Merry spent the afternoon picking up a few dishes, an air mattress, new sheets and a pillow so she could stay in her apartment until she had decided whether or not to accept Keith Owens's offer. She went ahead and had a telephone installed so she wouldn't have to rely completely on her cellular phone.

That night at Claire's she discussed the offer with Jason. His reaction was what she had expected. He wanted her to take the job.

He took her hand. "You've got my head spinning and I can't think about anything else except you and making love to you. There's something I was supposed to tell you days ago."

"Really? What's that?"

"Rob and I talked about setting a trap for Dorian. After our meeting, Rob talked to me alone and suggested that we could give you a small recorder. We'll find out when Dorian's leaving work or going to the Royal Diner and have you casually confront him. It'll be the two of you, but it will be daylight out in public with people around, and Rob and I will be watching so you won't be in danger."

"I'll do it tomorrow."

Jason ran his hand across his forehead. "Rob said you wouldn't be afraid."

"Why would I be afraid in public with you close at hand? Would you be afraid if you were the one to do it?"

"Hell, no, but that's different."

"I don't know why. You think I'm too weak to take care of myself?" she asked in a haughty voice, and Jason couldn't bite back a grin as he remembered how she had knocked him flat in the parking lot.

"Let's go home and let me check out your muscles."

She made a face at him. "Call Rob now and set something up. The sooner the better."

Jason sighed and shook his head. "I should have known what your reaction would be." He reached into his pocket and pulled out his cellular phone. In minutes he handed it to Merry.

"He wants to check things out with you. We're set."

He watched her while she listened and talked to Rob and all Jason could think about was taking her home. He wanted to talk her into coming back to the ranch with him. When had he ever had trouble talking a female into anything he wanted? Since he had met Merry. She could resist all his wiles. He reached across the table to run his fingers along her soft cheek. She returned the phone to him, and he talked to Rob, who said he would call back as soon as he talked to Sebastian, but they would plan on tomorrow afternoon when Dorian left work.

Jason put away the phone and stood to take her hand. "Let's dance."

He whispered endearments in her ear and then tried to talk her into going back to the ranch, but she was adamant about returning to her new apartment.

When he walked to the door of her apartment with her,

she turned to face him, and he realized she didn't even intend to invite him inside.

"Aren't you going to show me your apartment?"

"Not tonight. You won't like it because it doesn't have furniture in it."

"Come home with me," he said.

"We've been over that more than once. We need a little time and space. Or at least I do, and I think you should take a step back."

"That's crazy when I feel the way I do about you," he said, wrapping her in his arms. "You're not going to let me come in tonight?"

"No, I'm not."

"I love you, Merry."

Her heart thudded, and she wanted so badly to believe him, so badly to go home with him, but he had a history that worried her. "You were very convincing when I met you and you told me you never wanted to marry."

"I wish I had kept my mouth shut. Don't you know that I've fallen in love with you? It happens, Merry. Why can't you believe me?"

"I want to, and maybe I will, but I want us both to do a few things that are logical."

"Yeah? Well, where's logic in this?" He leaned down to kiss her, his mouth covering hers, opening it as his tongue touched hers. Her heart pounded and she stood on tiptoe and clung to him to kiss him back. She wanted him desperately, wanted him to really be in love with her and she poured herself into her kisses until they both were panting.

"Give me your key," he whispered.

She pushed against his chest. "As difficult as this is, I'm going to do what I said. I'll talk to you tomorrow, and tonight was fun." She unlocked her apartment, stepped inside and gazed into smoldering blue-green eyes that took her breath with blatant desire.

"'Night, Jason," she said, thinking it was the hardest

hadn't been there before. Nevertheless she stood fast in her determination to put some time and space between them to see if he really was in love. She settled back against the car seat and watched him drive.

He slowed to a stop in front of an office building across the street from Wescott Oil. "Wait in the lobby. Sebastian will call me when Dorian leaves his office. Then I'll call you. It'll give you time to go to the corner, cross the street and get to the front doors about the same time he does."

"Will do," she said cheerfully, but he gazed at her as solemnly as ever. She climbed out of the car and entered the building without looking back, knowing he would circle the block and park where he could watch the proceedings.

She stood waiting, glancing at her watch. It was thirty minutes after five, only five minutes since she'd last looked at the time. The sun was angled in the west and traffic had picked up on Main as people came out of offices to go home. The minute the high-pitched ring of her cellular phone came, she answered and heard Jason's voice.

"Sebastian said Dorian is leaving the building."

"I'm on my way."

"The recorder is on?"

"Yes," she replied, switching it on, still amused and touched by his concern. She was certain he had never been this way with any operatives he had worked with. "'Bye, Jason."

As she hurried out of the building and approached Wescott Oil, her pulse quickened. The glass doors reflected the sunlight, but most employees exited the back where the large employee parking lot was located. Only the executives could park near the front door. She kept walking toward the door, slowing because she would reach the front door before Dorian and she wanted it to look like a chance casual encounter out in front of the building.

And then Dorian strode through the door, sunlight catching glints in his brown hair. Dressed in a brown suit and tie, he was a handsome man who resembled his half brother, but there was something far kinder in Sebastian's usual expression than in Dorian's tight-lipped appearance.

She moved into Dorian's path, blocking the way, with the western sun behind her so he would be facing the sun. "Dorian," she said.

His gaze flew to hers and he stopped instantly.

Eleven

Briefly, she caught a flare of recognition in his eyes and then it was gone, but she knew she hadn't imagined it.

"I don't believe we know each other," he said curtly. "Should we?"

"Dorian, I'm Merry Silver, and we know each other very well."

"You must have mistaken me for someone else. Your reputation and actions precede you, Miss Silver, so of course, I do know you from your attacks on me. Am I safe or should I be screaming for help now?"

She moved a step closer, aware of a faint scent of his aftershave, remembering Jason's admonition to be careful. "You're safe enough from me. You know me and you know Holly. When you left, you broke her heart, and you were rotten to take her money."

"You do have the wrong person," he said with an infuriating calm. "This is the first time we've met, albeit I doubt if it will be the last, since you persist in laboring under a delusion.''

"There's no delusion, Dorian, and you know it.''

"There are laws to protect people like me from people like you. You can't run around accosting me. I can go from here to the sheriff's office. The police are willing to protect people from stalkers.''

"I'm not stalking you, and we both know that, too, as well as we both knew each other in Dallas. I don't know why you're ignoring me or what purpose it serves you, Dorian, but the truth usually comes out.''

"I hope it does and you pack up and go home. Now, if you'll excuse me—'' he stated in an impassive voice. After that first flare of recognition, there had been nothing but coldness in his expression.

Frustration rocked Meredith. The man was blatantly lying, yet there was nothing she could do about it. Why would he continue to lie? Jilting Holly had nothing to do with what had happened in Royal.

"Dorian, tell the truth!'' she snapped.

"I'm going straight to the sheriff.''

"You can't do anything when all I've done is say hello.''

"I'm sorry for you and your poor deluded sister,'' he said. "Goodbye, miss.'' He started to walk away and all of Merry's frustration welled up. She shook with anger, clenching her fists more tightly.

"You're going to get caught,'' she said.

He looked over his shoulder at her and his eyes narrowed and for a few heart-stopping seconds, she felt a chill from the cold fury that glinted in his eyes. Then it was gone.

"I don't have any idea what you're babbling about, Miss Silver. I suggest you go home to Dallas before you end up in a psychiatric ward or in jail for stalking me.''

Turning, he strode past her to his car.

Merry watched helplessly, angry that she hadn't shaken him and he hadn't admitted one sentence of the truth.

She stood in the sunshine and watched Dorian climb into

his car in one of the Wescott executive parking slots. Through his car's tinted windows, he seemed to look into her eyes and it appeared that he smiled. She couldn't be certain.

Her fists were clenched and she was breathing hard. As they had agreed, she turned to walk to Claire's where she would meet Jason.

The moment she stepped into the restaurant's cool, quiet interior, she reached into the pocket of her suit to switch off the recorder. Claire's elegant interior and late-afternoon quiet was a relief to Merry. She realized that her nerves were stretched taut, and she took a deep breath, glancing beyond the entryway at the almost empty dining room with its linen-covered tables.

A minute later Jason came striding through the door. He was handsome, walking with an easy, self-assured stride, a faint smile on his face. At the sight of Jason, she forgot Dorian, her frustration and all the dashing of her hopes the past half hour had brought. She longed to walk into Jason's arms and hold him, to feel his strong arms around her.

"There you are," he said cheerfully, his easy-going, good nature having returned in full. "Have you been waiting long?"

"No, not at all," she answered, knowing that he knew exactly when she had walked into the restaurant, and she wondered why he was bothering to create a cover for what they had been doing. No one else except Dorian would know or care.

Jason brushed her cheek with a kiss, hugged her lightly. "Let me get us a table," he said quietly, and turned to talk to the maître d'.

In minutes they were seated in a corner, and Jason ordered chablis with appetizers of wild mushrooms with grated Asiago cheese. Looking at her over the plate of appetizers, he said, "I can tell—you struck out."

"Yes," she replied, scowling and not trying to hide what she felt. "I wanted to reach out and shake him."

"I'm glad you didn't. You know what I told you about goading him."

"I didn't touch him. He acted as if I was a total stranger to him. Not once did he say anything to indicate he had ever known me."

"The man's clever."

"But such a blatant liar!"

"If he's our man, he's done much worse than lie. When we leave here, I want to go to your apartment and hear the tape. Unless you'll come home with me and let me listen to it there?"

"You can come to my apartment," she said reluctantly, her thoughts still on Dorian. "I feel as though I've failed Holly again. And you."

"Don't be ridiculous. That was just one gambit and it didn't work." Tilting his head to one side, he studied her. "Do you know how long it's been since I kissed you?" he asked, and his voice lowered a notch.

She smiled. "About ten minutes ago when you came into the restaurant."

"I mean really kissed you, the way I want to," he replied in a husky voice that made her pulse beat faster.

"At my door after our date last night," she replied. "If that's the kind of kiss you're talking about."

"That's way too long," he said, taking her hand to brush warm kisses lightly over her knuckles. His kisses made her tingle as much as his words, and she forgot being with Dorian or the frustration she had been feeling. All her attention was on the breathtakingly handsome man gazing solemnly at her.

He raised his wineglass in a toast. "Here's to tonight."

She arched her brows and raised her glass to touch his. "Fine. What's tonight?"

"A special evening with you. Each one is a celebration of my love. I love you, Merry. Deeply, truly, always. Sooner or later you're going to realize that I'm telling the truth."

"Jason..." she said, turning to brush a kiss on the back of his hand.

Their roasted king salmon served with a lemon artichoke aioli arrived, and while they ate, Jason talked about his rodeo days when he was in college and immediately afterwards, keeping her laughing and her thoughts off Dorian and the afternoon.

"You and your brothers were a wild bunch!"

"I doubt if we were half as wild as your brother Hank."

"That's probably true. Hank has spent a few nights in jail for brawls. You probably charmed your way out of that."

"I don't recall charming too many cops, or having to charm them, either. And I seem to be striking out with you when it really counts."

She smiled at him. "You're not striking out at all. You're just not getting your way every single second."

"I'm not getting my way about anything where you're concerned."

"That's not true."

"I want you to marry me. I want you to come back home with me. I didn't want you to talk to Dorian today. Tell me when I get to something where I'm having my way."

She laughed. "Maybe you haven't been getting your way quite as much lately."

"I haven't gotten my way since I met you."

"I think you have, a few times. Like, what do you want to do right now?"

"Take you home and make love to you," he answered instantly.

"Then what are we waiting for?" she said, knowing she was breaking her own rule, but unable to resist him.

He was already on his feet and taking her arm. She smiled at him as she stood. He kissed her lightly and leaned close to whisper in her ear, "I could eat you up right here if you'd let me."

"Get going," she said, her heart racing in anticipation.

He slipped his arm around her waist as they left the restaurant.

At the door of her apartment, she put her hand against his chest. The May night was cool and beautiful with sparkling stars and a clear sky. Crickets chirped, but otherwise the apartment complex was quiet and far enough from Main that all sounds of traffic were muffled.

"We'll make love a little while, but I didn't mean you can stay the night."

"Merry, that's not—"

She placed her finger on his lips. "Take it or leave it."

"All right."

"And—" she added, and he groaned "—we'll listen to the recording first."

"How about last?"

"Nope. Cowboy, it's time you didn't get your way about a few things in life."

"Let's hear that damned tape, and then I want you in my arms."

"One more thing."

"Merry, stop it."

"You can't fuss about my apartment. I haven't decided whether I will take the job with Keith or not, so I don't want to furnish this until I make that decision. I'm quite comfortable living here, so don't tell me I should move back with you. Do you understand?"

"Lady, you've got more rules than the Texas Senate. But I know what I can do about yours. Come here." He hauled her into his arms and kissed her. The moment his tongue stroked hers, all of Merry's pent-up longing for him exploded. Her hands shook as she ran them over his shoulders and through his hair.

"Your key," he whispered, and kissed her before she could answer or think. When she held up her key, Jason took it from her without pausing in his kisses.

Merry didn't care, knowing only that he swung her into his arms, pushed open her door, and kicked the door shut behind him. He set her on her feet and began peeling away her clothing.

She removed his as swiftly, wanting him and knowing she was breaking all her promises to herself, yet how could she resist or stop him now?

"Where's your bed?"

"There isn't one. There's a mattress on my patio."

"The hell with that," he said between kisses and took her down on the bare floor with him to roll over and move her on top of him. Merry sat astride, letting him stroke and fondle and kiss her until he shifted her hips and eased her onto his hard shaft.

They rocked together, and she was in ecstasy, deeply in love with this wonderful man. They crashed over a brink. Release, rapture enveloped her and she sprawled over him, both of their bodies covered in a sheen of sweat.

Slowly, their breathing returned to normal. He stroked her back lightly, lifting her hair away from her face. She raised up slightly to look at him. "All right, you got your way again. What did I tell you?"

"Maybe I did this time, but it's only once out of a hundred times lately. He rolled her over beside him and looked beyond her. "Merry, this apartment doesn't have one—"

She put her fingers on his lips. "What did I tell you?"

"Okay. I'll try to keep quiet. I love you, lady. Really love you."

She hugged him, refusing to admit her feelings, knowing there hadn't been enough time to prove anything to her yet. She wriggled away and caught up her blouse. "I'm going to shower—alone. Then you shower, and then we'll listen to the recording. And no complaints from you, because for the last little while, you have certainly gotten your way."

He snagged her ankle. "Tell me you didn't like my way."

"I loved it," she admitted in a sultry voice. "Now let go."

"Merry, dammit, woman, I want you."

''I'll be back.'' She hurried to her small bathroom, shut and locked the door.

While Jason showered, Merry switched on kitchen lights, poured glasses of iced tea, took out the recorder and sat cross-legged on the floor. She had changed to cut-offs and a T-shirt, was barefoot and let her hair hang free.

Jason came into the kitchen. He wore only his jeans and her mouth went dry at the sight of him. She knew she was going to have to struggle to resist him during the next hour.

He crossed the room to her and the desire in his eyes made her hot and tingly and breathless. ''Tape,'' she reminded him, yet her word came out as a breathless whisper.

''Yeah, sure,'' he answered in a husky voice and sat down facing her, sliding his hand behind her nape to pull her to him and kiss her. When she pushed lightly against his chest, he finally stopped.

She switched on the tape, and Jason listened without comment until the end, when she told Dorian he was going to get caught.

''Oh, hell, Merry,'' Jason said.

''What? I just told him he would get caught.''

''Then he knows you think he's the murderer. There's nothing concerning Holly to get caught about.''

''Of course there is—taking her money.''

''That's old stuff now and it's her word against his unless you or Holly come up with some solid proof. Merry, don't goad him.''

''I was so angry—''

''Just cool it. This man could be incredibly dangerous. He doesn't know what or how much you know. I'm staying here tonight.''

''No, you're not.''

''I swear, I'll sit in the living room. I'm worried about you.''

She thought about the night the bomb exploded and nodded. ''All right. Tonight you stay. Tomorrow night you go home. But you stay in the living room and I sleep on the patio.''

''Nope. Not tonight. You sleep in your bedroom where he can't scale a wall and get to you.''

She shivered and rubbed her arms. ''You're worrying me.''

''Good. I'm glad something is finally worrying you about Dorian.''

She leaned back against the wall and stretched her legs in front of her while they talked about the murder and their suspicions, and conversation gradually changed to other times and places. She glanced at her watch and then stared hard in amazement. ''Jason, it's after four in the morning! I'm going to bed.''

''I thought you'd never ask me.''

''I didn't ask you,'' she said pushing against his chest. ''I'll sleep in my bedroom, and I don't have a spare air mattress.''

''I'm not going to sleep anyway.''

She didn't think it was necessary because security was good at the apartment complex, but she didn't argue, going to the patio to retrieve her mattress and then carrying it to her tiny bedroom.

She fell asleep thinking about Jason making love to her, holding her, showering her with attention and kisses.

The next morning when she awakened, he was gone. He'd left a note, and she read his large scrawl.

I think you're safe now, so I'm heading home. See you tonight.

With a smile she held his note against her heart. In a few minutes she would get up, but right now, she just wanted to remember the night and Jason.

That morning, Merry called Keith Owens to accept his job offer, and then she began to make arrangements to have her things moved from her apartment in Dallas to her new apartment in Royal.

Merry was no closer to feeling certain about Jason's declarations of love, but she knew she was miserable seeing less of him. Even so, she kissed him good night at the door Friday after their date and went inside to spend another evening alone.

She closed shutters and switched on a small lamp she'd bought, moving through the empty apartment, her steps echoing faintly as her heels clicked on the bare hardwood floor. She changed to a frilly red teddy, switched off the lamp and lay down on the air mattress. She had washed the new sheets and had them draped on the mattress, but it wasn't the same as being in Jason's arms in his big bed, held close against him.

She woke to a terrible racket. Disoriented, she opened her eyes, trying to get her bearings, and remembering the empty apartment.

A band was playing, and someone was singing loudly and off-key. And she recognized the voice.

Twelve

Shocked, she jumped up. As she looked around for clothing, her phone rang. She yanked up the receiver while she grabbed her cutoffs.

"Miss Silver," came the distraught voice of Willard Smythe, her landlord. "Jason Windover is in front singing—I think to you. Get him to stop immediately."

"I'm going," she said, half hearing the landlord, half listening to Jason's raucous rendition of "I'll Always Love You."

"I will give you two minutes, Miss Silver, to put a stop to this infernal cacophony before I call the sheriff. Of course, your neighbors may already have called him."

"I'm going," she said, and hung up, yanking up a T-shirt to pull over her head and jamming her feet into sneakers. *How could he?* "Jason, stop!" she muttered, pushing buttons to open the gates.

Flinging open the door, she raced toward the front gate. Lights spilled over the grounds, banishing the night.

"Stop," she said under her breath. Jason was exciting, intelligent, capable, handsome, so many good things, but he was definitely not a singer.

"Shut up!" some deep male voice yelled loudly.

She groaned and ran faster, stunned to see a band outside. Jason, dressed in jeans and a plaid Western shirt, held a mike and flowers, and was on his knee while he sang to her.

"I love you," he called when he saw her. "Will you marry me?"

"Jason, stop!" Sirens screamed in the distance, and in spite of the hour of the morning, a crowd was beginning to appear. As a flashbulb popped, she heard the drone of a helicopter. She had lived all her life with a mother who had a nose for news, and in minutes, Merry knew, they would be on television. In minutes beyond that, Jason would probably be in a police car charged with disturbing the peace.

"Marry me," he called again.

"Yes!" she yelled. "Just stop singing! Come here."

The band cheered and gathering onlookers applauded as Jason tossed aside the mike, stood and sprinted through the gates. He wrapped his arm around her waist.

"Let's go before they haul you to jail, or my family sees me on the morning news."

They raced for her apartment, running inside and slamming the door. Laughing, he wrapped his arms around her and held her.

"Jason, you're crazy!"

"I heard you say yes."

She could tell him she did it to get him to stop singing, that it was the desperation of the moment. Or she could take a risk, let go of her fears and caution, believe this tall Texan who had stormed into her life, and love him in return.

While he waited, his blue-green eyes searched hers. Taking a deep breath, she stood on tiptoe to wrap her arms around his neck. "You get your way, cowboy, but you better mean what you say when you tell me you love me. When I marry, I want it to be forever."

"You'll marry me?"

"Yes, Jason, I'll marry you," she said firmly. "I love you."

"Ahh, Merry," he said, letting out his breath. "You've made me the happiest man on earth," he added before he leaned down to kiss her and end all conversation.

Midmorning he held her close against him, propping himself on his elbow to look down at her. "This is a hell of a thing to sleep on."

"I don't recall much sleeping since you arrived."

"Maybe not, but let's move back to my ranch."

"Not until we're married."

"Lordy, how long to I have to wait?" he asked, groaning.

"We both have families, and I'm the first child to marry in mine and my mother will want a big celebration."

"You'll set up vacation time?"

"I will, Keith said I can work at home, so my work hours will still be somewhat flexible. Of course, after last night, I may be evicted from this place."

"I'm sure you'll smooth it over and charm that stuffy landlord of yours. He pranced out and warned me he was calling the police."

"Which didn't scare you at all. Jason, that was really low."

"My singing is that bad? Don't answer. I know it is. I was desperate without you." He stretched out his arm and pulled his jeans close to search a pocket, withdrawing something. He took her hand and looked at her.

"Sure? It wasn't just to stop my singing?"

"I'm sure," she replied solemnly. He slid the dazzling ring on her finger while he kissed her, and in minutes she forgot her new ring as she wrapped her arms around Jason to love him in return.

Epilogue

The last weekend in May, Jason stood at the front of the church with Ethan, his oldest brother, beside him as best man. Luke, his other brother, Rob, Sebastian and another longtime friend, Matt Walker, were groomsmen. Jason had cajoled Merry into a hasty wedding, but both had the resources to hire enough people to help pull it together quickly. And, to his delight, Merry seemed as eager as he was.

Jason watched bridesmaids come down the aisle, friends and sisters of Merry's he had met at parties and seen again at the rehearsal last night. Holly was maid of honor. He had been surprised to find she was a beautiful young woman, several inches taller than Merry, with the same wide, smokey eyes and flawless skin. Several of the single guys from home had taken to her quickly, and Jason was glad to see that she had gone out with one of them the night before the rehearsal, then last night after the rehearsal she'd left with Porter Hammons, a cowboy from Royal who was one of the ushers for the wedding.

At the sound of a peal of music, Merry's mother stood and turned, and everyone else came to their feet, but from that moment on, Jason was aware only of Merry, who came down the aisle toward him on the arm of one of her uncles.

Her hair was piled on her head, hidden mostly by the gossamer white veil. She was radiant, glowing with love, taking his breath in her long, white dress, and then she was beside him, her hand in his as they repeated their vows.

As he promised to love, honor and cherish her the rest of his life, the vows seemed so right, something he had already promised her more than once in intimate moments. Now he felt as though he had waited all his life for her, the perfect woman for him.

"You may kiss your bride," the minister said, and Jason turned back her veil, looking into her eyes filled with warmth and love. He leaned down to brush her lips lightly, and then they walked back up the aisle together, Mr. and Mrs. Jason Windover, which sounded wonderful to him.

"I've got you, babe," he whispered in her ear as they entered the foyer.

"And I've got you, Jason. I love you."

"Let's cut this reception short."

"Be patient. This is a once-in-a-lifetime, and I want to enjoy dancing with you."

He grinned, wrapped his arm around her waist, and they went through a hallway to go back around to the front of the church to pose for pictures.

The reception was at a country club where Merry's mother was a member. To Merry's surprise, her brother, Hank, had come home for her wedding. She watched as he stood talking to Jason, suspecting Jason might be a good influence in Hank's life.

She studied her handsome husband, and her heart raced in anticipation of their honeymoon. In a black tux, Jason was incredibly handsome, and she had to struggle to pay attention to friends and relatives and mingle in the crowd.

She saw Holly surrounded by a cluster of guys from Royal. They had discovered her during parties there, and to Merry's enormous relief, Holly seemed to have forgotten Dorian.

"Your sister is having a good time."

Merry looked around to see Susan Wescott. "Yes, she is. It's funny how things turned out. She's getting over Dorian, I'm married to Jason now—"

"That day we met at the Cattleman's Club, I thought you were going to take the place by storm," Susan said, smiling, her silver-gray eyes holding a twinkle.

"I don't want to think about that," Merry said. "I was dreadful."

"They deserved to get their staid old club shaken up a little," Susan said. "I wish you and Jason the best. When you can, I want both of you to come visit."

"Thanks, Susan. I'd love that," Merry said, realizing she had a friend. Someone called to Susan, who moved away, sunlight catching red glints in her chestnut hair.

Merry thought about Dorian, who still raised so many unanswered questions. Her marriage to Jason had to have angered Dorian, particularly since she was determined to find out if he'd been involved in murdering Eric Chambers and trying to frame Sebastian.

Jason was talking to a circle of tall, handsome men, all members of the Texas Cattleman's Club. It was a diverse and close-knit group. Some of the men she had just met for the first time: ranchers Matt Walker and Forrest Cunningham; Blake Hunt; a doctor named Justin Webb; Sheikh Ben Rassad; Hank Langley; Dakota Lewis, a retired air force lieutenant; Greg Hunt, a lawyer; Sterling Churchill. Others she had met before: Aaron Black, Keith, Rob, Sebastian and Will Bradford.

While they talked, Jason looked around the circle of men,

well aware that Dorian had been excluded, yet feeling not one shred of remorse.

"Well, Keith, we ought to plan the ball and you better start thinking about the charity you want, because you are the last bachelor standing," Jason drawled with a smile.

"I can't believe I've won this. I never thought I'd see this happen," Keith grinned and replied to Jason, gesturing to include the reception festivities.

"Our playboy retires," Rob stated.

"It's about time," Aaron added. "Next thing you know, the playboy will be announcing a baby on the way."

Jason grinned, unable to stop smiling. "I leave the bachelor and playboy reputation to Keith, who outlasted all the rest of us."

All the men chimed in and Aaron raised his glass. "Here's a toast to the man who keeps bachelorhood alive in Royal—our own Keith Owens. Our confirmed old bachelor."

"All right, you guys. We'll see who has the most fun at that ball," Keith answered with a laugh.

"I know who will," Jason said, "all the married guys. Each of us will get to take home the woman he loves."

"To the women in our lives," Sebastian said, proposing another toast and immediately glasses were raised.

"What's your charity going to be?" Aaron asked Keith as they lowered their glasses.

"Y'all told me to think about it and I have," Keith said. "I've picked what I want."

"Tell us what it is," Jason said.

"The New Hope Charity for battered women," he said quietly.

And Jason nodded while Aaron said, "That's a good charity."

Others repeated Aaron's sentiments while Jason thought about Keith's old flame from college. If he remembered correctly, Andrea O'Rourke was a volunteer at New Hope.

"And how long is this honeymoon?" Rob asked, bringing Jason's thoughts back to the present. Jason realized there was a serious note in Rob's voice.

"Only a week and I will leave word with you—and only you—how you can get in touch with me if there is an emergency."

As all of them sobered, Jason suspected each one of them was thinking about Dorian.

"When you get back, we'll have another meeting and see where we go from here. There's still nothing that really pins anything on him," Rob stated.

"Even if it did, he has an alibi," Jason said, aware they didn't even have to say Dorian's name.

"If any of you need any kind of help from more of us," Aaron offered, "you know we'll be glad to do whatever we can."

"Thanks. Now, my friends, I think I'll go find my bride and I'll see y'all when we get back to Royal."

Jason and Merry left Royal, driving to Dallas to the bridal suite in an elegant hotel. Tomorrow they had a flight to Madrid, and then they were driving to a small town on the Mediterranean coast of Spain.

The moment the door closed behind the bellman, Jason reached for Merry to pull her into his arms. He still wore his tux, but she had changed to a simple navy dress and pumps. His arms tightened around her and he leaned down to kiss her.

"Mrs. Jason Windover. I've got you, love, and you'll see how much I mean it when I tell you I love you."

"Your playboy days are over, Jason."

"I was just waiting for you, darlin'. You're the one and only in my life forever."

He bent his head to kiss her and Merry stood on tiptoe, wrapping her arms around his neck as she clung to him and kissed him in return. Joy filled her, and she no longer had any doubts about the depth of Jason's love. And she didn't intend him to have any doubts about the depth of her love for him. She loved him with all her being, and she planned to spend a lifetime showing him so. She tightened her arms around his neck, whispering, "I love you, my special cowboy."

* * * * *

Watch for the next installment of the
TEXAS CATTLEMAN'S CLUB:
THE LAST BACHELOR
*When millionaire executive Keith Owens runs
into his old flame, Andrea O'Rourke, even
the last bachelor standing may go down for
the count. Can Keith convince the woman of
his dreams to take another chance on love?*
THE BACHELOR TAKES A WIFE
by Jackie Merrit
*Coming to you from Silhouette Desire
in June 2002.*
And now for a sneak preview of
THE BACHELOR TAKES A WIFE,
please turn the page.

One

___

Keith Owens was well aware of Jason Windover's air of contentment as he and his friends prepared cups of coffee for themselves at a serving cart, then sat in comfortable chairs around a table in one of the Cattleman's Club's private meeting rooms. Jason good-naturedly laughed off the teasing remarks about his and Merry's honeymoon, from which they'd returned only the day before, because it was all in fun and he'd expected some tongue-in-cheek banter from his buddies. But he wasn't above giving back at least part of what he was getting. And Keith, being the only bachelor remaining in the group, naturally seemed to be his best target.

"Just you wait, old pal," Jason drawled. "Some sweet lookin' little gal is out there this very minute, just biding her time for the right moment to rope and hog-tie Royal's most elusive executive."

"Elusive executive?" Keith repeated with a laugh, and looked around the table for confirmation or denial from

Sebastian Wescott, William Bradford, Robert Cole and, of course, Jason, all of whom wore big smiles. "Is that what I am?"

"Sounds like an apt description to me," Sebastian said. "Good work, Jason."

"Thanks," Jason said with a cocky grin at Keith.

"All right, I get it," Keith said. "I'm the last bachelor among you jokers, and you're not going to let me forget it. Well, put this in your pipes and smoke it, old friends. I happen to enjoy bachelorhood."

"So did we when we were young and foolish," Rob said with an overly dramatic sigh.

Everyone laughed, because they'd *all* been bachelors only five months ago and they'd been neither young nor foolish. Only one thing had happened to change their status from single to married—falling in love, which was a mighty powerful force they had discovered. And not a man around that table, other than Keith, believed that Royal's "exclusive executive" would remain a bachelor for long. After all, hadn't he already tossed his hat in the ring by naming New Hope Charity for battered women as the beneficiary of the Cattleman's Club's annual charity benefit? That decision, made by Keith, was going to bring Andrea O'Rourke, his old college flame, back into his life, since she was the volunteer at New Hope who dealt firsthand with public donations. It seemed to the men around the table that if Keith hadn't wanted contact with Andrea, then he would have named an entirely different charity to receive this year's check.

No one said so, though, as some subjects weren't up for open and verbal conjecture. They could tease Jason, because he'd just come back from his honeymoon, but they couldn't make light of Keith's sudden interest in renewing ties with Andrea.

"Much as I'm enjoying this, I think it's time we got down to the reason we called this meeting. Dorian." The other four friends sobered at once. They all shared the strong suspicion that Dorian Brady had murdered Eric Chambers, an accountant at Wescott Oil. But so far, they had no proof of his involvement.

Keith began. "We've been doing our best to keep an eye on Dorian during your absence, Jason, and none of us have spotted anything suspicious. In fact, it appears that if anything, Dorian has been deliberately maintaining a low profile."

"That's suspicious in itself," Jason said. "Don't you agree, Sebastian?"

"Dorian was never low-key before," Sebastian soberly agreed. He was understandably more affected by recent events than the others, since Dorian was his half brother. "Except when it fit his agenda. As you all know, his showing up out of the blue was one hell of a shock. We look so much alike, I never for a minute doubted his story about Dad being his father, and I still don't. Putting him to work at Wescott Oil was a bad error in judgment, however. My only excuse was that I really wanted to help him."

"None of what happened is your fault, Sebastian," Keith said quietly. "How do honest people deal with a snake like Dorian? He's deliberately gone out of his way to undermine your authority and good reputation with the company and the community in general. Don't blame yourself for anything Dorian's done."

"Considering his background with Merry's sister even before coming to Royal, he's a louse without anyone else's help or good intentions gone astray," Jason said stonily. No one could disagree with that summation, and the conversation changed directions.

"What we still can't figure out is his motive for murder. What was Eric Chambers to him, other than a coworker? It simply doesn't add up."

Sebastian got up for a coffee refill. "I've wrestled with that since the murder, and I have a hunch that it's all connected to me. Jason, I know you were uneasy about

Dorian from the start." Sebastian resumed his seat. "Why?"

"We've covered this ground before," Keith said.

"Yes, but obviously we're missing something," Sebastian persisted. He frowned slightly and added, "What could it be?"

"His computer files imply that Dorian was blackmailing Eric," Jason reminded them. "Merry discovered that."

"Yes, but those files do not explain a cause for blackmail. What was Eric up to that Dorian was able to discover and use against him? Maybe if we knew more about Eric," he mused. "What do we really know about him?"

"He worked for Wescott for quite a few years," Sebastian volunteered. "He was a very private individual with a cat as his only companion. He was divorced long before coming to work for Wescott, so no one I know has ever met his ex. He lived alone...with his cat...in a small house. That struck me as odd because he made a good annual salary."

"Which he could have been paying to his ex-wife in alimony," Keith said.

"But he wasn't. His wife had remarried quite a while back, ending the alimony payments, and there were no children for Eric to support. He could've afforded a better home, considering his earning power."

"Follow the money," Jason said, half in jest.

But the simple concept simultaneously struck all five men as critically important. They looked at each other, and several of them nodded. Months ago money had been missing at Wescott Oil. Sebastian, accused of killing Eric and taking the money—a ridiculous charge when he owned the company and had more money than he could ever spend—had been completely exonerated and all charges against him had been dropped. Since then, everyone had been concentrating on Eric's murder. The missing money was still unexplained, a loose end left dangling.

It could be the clue they had been hoping to uncover and follow up on.

presents

A brand-new miniseries about the Connellys of Chicago,
a wealthy, powerful American family tied by blood to the
royal family of the island kingdom of Altaria.
They're wealthy, powerful and rocked by
scandal, betrayal...and passion!

Look for a whole year of glamorous and
utterly romantic tales in 2002:

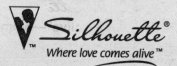

Where love comes alive™

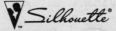

If you enjoyed what you just read, then we've got an offer you can't resist!

Take 2 bestselling love stories FREE!

Plus get a FREE surprise gift!